1·25
22

Hell Hath No Sorrow like a Woman Haunted

PRAISE FOR HELL HATH NO SORROW LIKE A WOMAN HAUNTED

"In Hell Hath No Sorrow, looming over the individual abusers, monsters, and decent people who make mistakes, is another more sinister threat: our patriarchal culture immersed in violence and racism. This comes across most damningly in the final story in the collection, "Into the Nothingness." Though monsters are terrifying, the supposedly mundane world is the most haunted thing Joseph's characters (and all of us) must face." – H.V. Patterson

PRAISE FOR RJ JOSEPH

"Bloodline" (*Monstrous Domesticity*) – "Nothing like a creepy family with creepy rules and secrets to keep a reader interested! It's hard to say much about this story without giving it all away, so that one sentence shall have to suffice." - Once Upon a Tome

"Black Like That" (*Dead Inside*) – "A short poem about the blackness that lurks beneath the surface. The imagery on offer lives long in the memory." - Ross Jeffery

"The Collector" (*Slash Her*) – "One of the darkest stories I've ever read. Still a bit shook." - Thomas Gloom

"Left Hand Torment was absolutely mind-shattering for me. That's the only one that honestly, gave me nightmares; it was so terrifying, hauntingly vivid, and brutal. I thoroughly enjoyed it…raw, more than viscerally violent content. It is definitely hardcore horror; these are the kinds of [stories] women in horror are sometimes accused of being too dainty in our sensibilities and sensitive to write." - Sumiko Saulson, editor of Black Magic Women

ALSO BY RJ JOSEPH

(where you can find stories not in this collection)

Slash Her: An Anthology of Women in Horror

The Dead Inside, A Horror Anthology

Under Her Skin, A Women in Horror Poetry Collection, 1

Diabolica Americana, A Dark States Horror Compendium

Twisted Anatomy: A Body Horror Anthology

Hell Hath No Sorrow like a Woman Haunted

RJ Joseph

Illustrated by
Robert Bose

THE SEVENTH TERRACE

HELL HATH NO SORROW LIKE A WOMAN HAUNTED
ISBN 13: 978-1-990082-18-4
The Seventh Terrace First Trade Paperback Edition - 2022

The Seventh Terrace
www.the-seventh-terrace.com

Dedicated to my village, without which I wouldn't be the writer I am. Y'all allow me to stay, dark heart and weird voices and all. Much love to you.

Sorrows

Foreword

Sometimes it's just right.

Sometimes the stars align and you are in the right place at the right time to meet someone, to find something, to experience something that will change your life. This change can come in any forms – blatant and stamped on your persona, or as a subtle shift in perspective. Whatever the impact, it something you know when you see (or feel) it; it is an "aha" moment that you grab by the tail before it flits away. Reading R J Joseph has been that epiphany for me. Whether in her academic essays relating to the monstrous feminine or her dark stories that hit closer to home than is comfortable, R J Joseph manages to bring to fore emotions that usually go unsettled, unaddressed, and undiagnosed... sometimes with good reason. Her uncanny ability to find the raw spot and caress it with a salt-coated fingernail is unnerving while at the same time intriguing. Her reflection of Black women in all of our flavors—our joys and pains and the strange intermingling of the two—is terrifying in its poignancy.

The stories in this collection breathe life into the body horror subgenre and dance along the edges of the extreme as they go 'round the carousel. Complex, visceral, and at times mesmerizing, these stories exist separate from each other but could be viewed as a whole, a mosaic of emotions related to motherhood, the process of aging, social constructs, partnership; the entire unit a kaleidoscopic projection of imagery related to the body feminine that shines a light on what lies beneath, what scurries away from view. Often love is at the root of the reflection, is what is exposed in the bright light, and what we are treated to isn't always pretty. The love between partners, the love of a mother for her children, unrequited love, what lengths will be travelled to gain someone's love, even the love of one's self is laid bare between these pages and readers may find their personal plights there, written in the blood that no one noticed has spilled. R J Joseph's ability to spin a yarn that the reader can find home in, the way her voice can take up residence in your own head such that seems like you are speaking to yourself, consoling yourself, celebrating, suffering, emboldening, is masterful. You know something is good when you twist in your seat in response, when your palms begin to sweat, when you respond audibly to a sentiment written on the page. This collection of enigmatic and colorful stories hits that way, hard and fast like a sucker punch, but one that your soul saw telegraphed in the ether. The stories are organic, responses to the very real horrors of life they speak of—the ones that are emblazoned on our very souls—and that realism makes them resonate even more... makes them hurt in the most fantastic of ways.

R J Joseph is an author with her finger on the pulse of the feminine experience. Her writing, the absolute purity of the emotions on the page... this is the tone of voice that horror needs to tell Black female stories. I could pick favorites – indeed, I am tempted to, but to do so might color your reading, so I will simply say this: every story brings a vantage point that veers from center, that makes you look inside yourself, that makes you nod you head in collective understanding. Here you will find stories that speak of realities, scenarios, mindsets, and practices that are only whispered about in mixed company – some that may never see the light of day in others. You will be treated to thought processes that may have arisen in you or other women in your life—these thoughts were likely never voiced or acted upon, but they reside still in the recesses of your mind. You will be shown things you've never seen before; you will have your attention turned in directions it has never lingered... and you will be frightened by what you see there. And that is ok. It is all by design, this revelatory collection, and you will arrive at the ending unscathed... but not unchanged. From the first story herein the change begins, working its way through your mind, body, and soul.

R J Joseph's stories provide a catharsis that has nothing to do with the natural course of healing: instead, it traverses another plane where retribution for wrongs is paramount and rest is not granted until it is achieved. This plane exists within all of us and that is what makes her stories eerily relatable... and utterly terrifying.

Read at your own risk. There's something amazing inside for the brave.

L. Marie Wood

Martinsburg, West Virginia

March 13, 2022

Left Hand Torment

I was on door duty that evening, though we didn't need a protector. Most passersby tended not to notice our nondescript entryway in the worn-down building. Even those who did notice it were deterred by the dark cloak of misery in our eyes. Despite my queerness and my race, those doorways to my soul, that broadcast unspeakable rot, allowed me kinship with the men inside. Her eyes held the same blackness, despite their light gray color, announcing her as kindred, serving as her password into the club.

There was more to her life story than her eyes, apparently. The foulness of whatever tortured her spirit bubbled just underneath the surface. Her dusky skin shone with determination and...fury. She glided ahead of me up the stairway and into the parlor, removing long white gloves as we walked. Severe burns covered both hands, the puckered skin reflecting the lantern lights.

Even Whitson, the resident playboy, did not set his flirtations upon her. He simply asked her what she was drinking, the same as he did the rest of us. He often told us that he did not seek companionship with fellow sufferers. He said their beds were already too full with them and their demons.

"Bourbon, please." The rich tones slid from her throat and escaped into the quiet murmur of the fifteen of us. She accepted her glass gracefully and settled into a chair close to the fireplace.

Not forgetting our Texas manners, we quieted down and allowed the lady the floor. I watched her sip from her glass.

"Merci." She accented the appreciation with a brisk nod to the side. When she gazed back at us, the flames from the fire flickered around the shadows resting beneath the smoky orbs of her haunted eyes. She pulled her bonnet off and placed it on the table next to the chair. Kinky curly strands spilled down to her shoulders and the room gave a collective gasp as the flames caught the sandy tresses. This was the only acknowledgement we gave to her beauty that night.

Without preamble, she spoke in accented tones. "My name is Dominique Aimee Beaulieu and I was born and reared in New Orleans. I had an ordinary childhood, if that as the daughter of a placee` on Rampart street could be called such. Papa and Maman loved me very much and I was a rather spoiled child. They loved each other, as well. I know Papa loved her more than he loved his wife. But he could not stay with us all the time. I once asked Maman why he had to leave and stay away so often and she explained to me that we could not be selfish and keep him all to ourselves. He had another family with whom he had to stay most of the time, but he was always thinking of us.

"Maman had a picture of a beautiful woman with blond hair and she often gazed wistfully at it when she thought Papa and I weren't looking. I would ask her about the woman, whose features I saw staring back at me in the mirror, albeit through darker skin. Maman would evade the answer until I turned sixteen. When I finally got my answer, I also got the explanation for our way of life.

"*This is my sister, your aunt. Papa's other wife. He met me as he courted her and wanted me for his left-hand wife. She knows about us but cannot acknowledge us publicly. But she must accept our existence. You are of courting age now. Papa will arrange for you to attend The Quadroon Ball next year, to find you a wealthy, white husband. Do not waste yourself frivolously on any colored man. Even if he has money, he can't elevate your status or guarantee that your children will be free men.*

"She grabbed my hand. *Just take care to always respect your husband and do his bidding. Love and honor him despite the feelings of jealousy that will come when he takes another to wife. We are the wives they choose, when their other will be chosen for them through making familial alliances. These arrangements are our only way to freedom.*

"I didn't understand why she beseeched me so dramatically on these points. Our system of placage was shocking enough to discover without her telling me I had to accept it, that I had few other choices. I knew nothing of love between a man and woman, but I could see the love between Maman and Papa. If it meant she had to share him with her sister, did that make it of any less value? Did that make me, the product of their left-hand union, any less valuable? Of course, I would love my husband, legally bound or not, because of all the things I did not understand, there was one thing I knew and never wanted to change: my freedom."

She paused her story here, seeming to look at us for the first time. She turned her fierce gaze on each of us, one at a time, her fellow beasts of demonic burdens. She settled her gaze finally on me, the lone other woman in the group. I did not know how I understood that she knew my secret. My fellow club members knew and did not care. "You understand when I say fighting for one's freedom is a frantic battle when losing means losing your personhood and often, your very life."

I nodded. I did know what a constant fight for freedom to simply exist required. Dying was preferable to giving in to bondage of any kind, hence my membership there. These, my brothers in terror, did not make anything big over my masculine clothes and obviously feminine body. My haunted heart bore witness to more important things to them. The rest of the world did have problems with me, as soon as my "charade" was discovered. I sought to fool no one. I simply loved other women and eschewed dresses and other frilly clothing. However, explaining that this was simply who I am would likely do nothing but result in a trail of bodies, raped to prove a point and beaten to force submission as was required of women—killed to salvage masculine and familial pride. Thus far, my own body did not increase those numbers of dead. As to the other tortures, I was a first-hand witness.

"I was excited about my first ball. Maman fussed over my dress and hair and Papa fussed about the shortage of eligible men he deemed worthy of his daughter. He finally settled on two men from prominent families who would arrive at the hall under the cover of night, just as the other attendees would.

"It is difficult to gain full understanding of a person through a portrait and word of mouth about his family, but I felt an attraction to the first man before I met him in person. I told Papa I wanted to meet and dance with him first, and as much as indulgence was against the proceedings, my Papa gave in.

"His name was Alesandre Pasquet. He nodded to Papa to request permission to dance with me. From the moment his hand touched mine, I felt panicked. Strange and uncomfortable feelings bubbled up inside me. They were frightening and unsettling in a way I was not prepared for. The closer Alesandre moved against my body, the more I wanted to pull away from him. The way my womb ached and my nether regions melted created an imbalance inside me. Maman had told me nothing of this when she explained these things to me. I could not catch Papa's eye for guidance. I thought I would swoon.

"And then Rene was there. He looked like a fallen angel with his dark hair worn just a bit longer than was fashionable, one curly lock falling over his eye. I felt an immediate sense of calm, discomfort gone in an instant. I looked into his dark eyes and found nothing there that explained...anything. *May I, Pasquet?*

"I was grateful for the rescue but did not overlook the fact that the question was not a question at all. Alesandre put up no fight and simply left me standing in the middle of the floor with Rene, as he fled. Sweat broke out onto his forehead and he stumbled backwards, eyes opened wide. I felt no pity towards him, nor any curiosity over the dealings between love rivals.

"*Please do not think me forward,* my rescuer began, *but you look quite terrified. Would you like to sit and have a drink?*

"I fell into his eyes, those bottomless brown pools of serenity. He placed his hand on my bare arm and led me back to where Papa sat. My sire was apoplectic. *Who are you and what are you doing with my daughter?*

"*I am Rene Fanchon Villemont Duplanchier. I am pleased to make your acquaintance.* Papa had no further fight, returning to his seat next to me. Trickles of sweat ran down his neck, and I had not seen them before I had left him moments before. He struggled with something, barely restrained. I had seen this expression before when workmen sought to cheat him when doing home repairs, or when passersby subjected Maman to insults as they walked on the streets. In those instances, he confronted the offenders. At that time, I was left to question what had engaged his ire.

"Rene returned with a glass of punch. *Mr. Beaulieu, may I walk with your beautiful daughter on the balustrade?* Papa barely nodded without speaking or moving otherwise. The sweat flowed faster. His eyes communicated something…sadness, maybe…and I thought him lost in reverie over my imminent engagement, as it was. It was clear at that point that I would become Rene's left-hand wife.

"My savior took me for a round in the cool night air. No words passed between us, and that comforted me. There were no terrible feelings bubbling up inside me, threatening to break out of my skin. He did not try to touch me, which was good, because my skin still ached deliciously from where he had touched my arm earlier. At the end of the stroll, he returned me to Papa and stated that he would call for me and make the final arrangements for our alliance.

"I went to bed that night with dreams of my own household and a calm, beautiful husband. I was awakened by Maman and Papa's argument.

"*You cannot let her go to that…that…demon!* Maman never raised her voice at Papa and she never went against his wishes.

" *We cannot stop it. He has placed his mark upon her. He will let no one else have her.* Papa sounded defeated, smaller than I had ever imagined. I tiptoed from my room to eavesdrop with a visual advantage.

"*I will place this gris-gris upon her. It will work. I know a woman in the Quarter who can help.* Maman spoke mostly to herself. Papa rocked ceaselessly in his chair, his despondent façade placing an ache in my heart that rivaled that of my arm.

"*We won't deal with that slave magic. She must go. To try to prevent him will be the sure destruction of…all of us.*

"Maman exploded. *So, it is your other children you are fearful for? You worry for your other wife, the one who does not love you as I do? The one who has your legal heirs?* Her mane of curly, ebony hair flared around her head like a crown of fury, unleashed from her headscarf.

"She dropped down next to his chair, unwilling to be defeated. *Please, Dominique is all I have. You cannot sacrifice her. You cannot.*

"Papa remained silent, stroking her back as she sobbed loudly. I went back to my room, confused about their talk of sacrifices. I fell into a fitful slumber, dreaming with no remembrance.

"As promised, Rene called at the townhouse the next day. *Mr. Beaulieu, Mrs. Beaulieu. I have come to make arrangements for Dominique's hand.* He stood on the townhome stoop, hat in hand.

"*No.* Maman whispered the word so that I had to come further down the hallway to hear her.

"Rene tilted his head, the expression on his face never changing.

"*If we do not invite you in, you cannot cross over our threshold.* Papa stood behind her, his hands on her shoulders. He restrained her as she moved in the direction of the door.

"*I will get the invitation I need. Dominique?*

"I had thought myself nearly invisible around the door, standing deep in the bowels of our house. I moved to the door in slippered feet, forgetting the decorum of receiving male guests only at the permission of Papa and Maman.

"*Dominique! No!* Maman moved towards me and halted, mid-step. Papa, drenched in sweat, also froze. Tears welled in Maman's eyes. *Where is your gris-gris, beloved?*

"I had removed the pouch from my neck at the end of the hallway. I arrived at the door and stretched my hand out to Rene. He smiled and walked into the living room.

"*We will not be staying. Tell your parents goodbye. We will be married at once and will retire in our own home tonight.*

"*Goodbye, Maman and Papa.* Rene did not release my hand, but I was not returning to my parents. I belonged to Rene. I spared one glance behind us as we departed, barely a fleeting thought given to the tears that flowed down my parents faces as they stood in the same places.

"True to his word, Rene and I went directly to the church and were married. I hardly remember the ceremony, thinking only of being with Rene. I napped as the carriage rode across New Orleans to my new home."

Dominique paused again, here, to sip her bourbon. She must have intuited the rules of our club and that we would wait patiently until she resumed her story. She took long moments, lost in her reverie. When she spoke again, her voice lowered.

"Rene did not come to me in the bedroom I occupied alone until after I had been there for three weeks. Then, he sent a note to request permission to come one night. In the three weeks' time, I had become acquainted with the servants, learning as much as I could from them about my new home. My husband had informed me that I could have the run of the house and that once I decided on décor items, he would send into town for them.

"The servants tried to prepare me for my imminent marital bed duties. I explained that my Maman had already done her job, but one woman, Nan, insisted.

"You do not understand, Mistress. You must be ready when he comes to you. I can help you. Her eyes begged me to give permission.

"Instead, I laughed. *I will be fine, Nan. This is what wives have done since the beginning of time.*

"She nodded, sadness overtaking her eyes. I felt bad about hurting her feelings, but I wanted everything to start on a positive note with my new husband. I already held some trepidation at the fact he had waited so long. I wanted everything to go naturally so we could start our intimate journey with no obstacles.

"I did allow her to help me bathe and rub scented oil over my body. I sat up in the bed to await his visit. My heart pounded when I bid him to enter the room. Under the candlelight, his beauty took my breath away. The same giddiness that had overtaken me at the ball almost a month earlier with Alesandre bubbled up in my womb.

"My husband floated with the shadows in the flames and slid under the coverlets I clutched in my hands.

"Are you afraid? He cupped my chin in his hands, and my body heated up. I had a hard time breathing.

"Becoming frantic, I nodded. I tried to scoot away, but he held my face in place.

"Do you wish me to make you comfortable?

"I nodded again.

"I have to hear the words, he prompted.

"Yes, please. I wish for comfort.

"Rene held my gaze and calm washed over me. My languid body slid down flat on the bed. He rose above me and without warning, pressed himself into my body. I felt the pain Maman and Nan had warned be about, but I could not react to it. My body would not move, even as my mind willed it to do so. But that was nothing compared to what was to come.

"Suddenly, my body was punctured by spikes that assaulted my canal as Rene moved in a rhythm inside of me. His member grew larger and the spikes stabbed me from within. I screamed inside my head and felt the blood rush through my veins as fear pumped through me just as Rene pumped. He did not require any movement from me as he took his pleasure.

"The torment I felt reflected from my eyes into his, as I tried to understand what was happening. My womb burned and wept, tissue tearing and trying, but failing, to accommodate the assault. He tilted my hips upward, because I could not move them, and he plundered my depths with searing strokes. I knew I would pass out from the pain.

"But then Rene spoke. *No. Stay here. You must receive me. You will bear my spawn.* Despite the overwhelming pain, my eyes remained open. Tears rolled down the sides of my head, my mouth silent as my brain sought refuge in delusion.

"All I could feel underneath my buttocks was warm, thick wetness. My blood bathed us in the virginal bed, marking the loss of my innocence. And my sanity.

"At the end of his attack, I felt something further up inside my body split. Rene held his position and his eyes changed. I felt movement that was not him. It felt like thousands of tiny feet trampling through my birth canal, upwards to my womb, to the very core of my body. From a mental distance, I worried that ants had become attracted to the blood Rene had drawn from me and had made their way into the bed.

"Those were not ants. They were his seeds, marching from his body, into mine, seeking fertile grounds in which to implant themselves. Up and up and up into my canal, they moved, relentless in their quest. My stomach heaved with nausea, and Rene focused his gaze on me, once again. The convulsions stopped, but the marching went on and on.

"They invaded the end of my opening, and swarmed outward, beyond just the area they were supposed to inhabit. I felt them marching through the tears in my tissues, gnawing their way through veins and muscles, planting themselves wherever they could.

"I had almost succeeded in leaving my body when Rene withdrew from me. Wetness flowed and flowed from the wound he left and did not say anything. I still could not move my body or scream, and fresh tears joined the fluids down below.

"Nan appeared at the bedside and she propped my legs up on extra pillows she must have brought into the room with her. I wanted to scream, but I could not even move my head to beg her to help me. The despair in her eyes as she tried to position me told me more than I wanted to know about my condition.

"She crossed herself and scurried about the room. She left and came back with an arm full of things. No longer able to stand the pain, I passed out.

"My own screams brought me to consciousness. Nan was there, shaking her head as she pressed warm cloths between my legs. I screamed again as the fabric barely grazed raw tissue. She murmured and took something from around her neck and pressed it into the cloth. All the pain did not go away, but I was able to elevate my thoughts above the pain. My body was a mangled mess I sought to escape.

"I did not see Rene again for another month. In that time, my wounds healed superficially, but my mind had grown further damaged. I did not understand as Nan tended to me and clucked, 'He must be stopped'. I agreed, but I did not know how to stop him. He was my husband. I was unable to leave the room, much less, the house. I was a prisoner.

"When Rene came again, I trembled in fear against the headboard. *Please. I cannot. I am still in great pain.*

"Rene did not heed my pleas. The torture began anew, ripping tender tissue that had barely begun to fuse together. Again, I was paralyzed on the surface. Whenever he closed his eyes, I began to feel the paralysis wear thin. That next assault was physically unbearable. I learned to look into his eyes without looking. My spirit left my body until he was done. Sometimes I did not allow it to return until weeks after the assault.

"The pain took on a different aspect after that second attack. I became bloated. I thrashed around in the bed, screaming, for many hours out of a day's time. Nan still tended to me, shaking her head and wringing her hands, consulting with other servants in hushed tones.

"One night, she awakened me and whispered fervently, *You carry his spawn. Those creatures cannot be borne.* I had no reason to question her. I knew she was right. I felt the creatures gnawing on the internal structures of my body. The constant pain made me delirious, and I stayed away from my physical prison more often than I remained conscious.

"But Nan's observation pushed me to action. I begged her to help me move around the bulk of my belly and get to the hallway. Once I reached the top of the stairway, I waved her away. That action would be mine, alone. I threw my body down the stairs, the bumps and collisions mild compared to what I had already endured. I prayed that I would die along with the monsters that my body hosted.

"I was not so lucky. I survived the fall. I was no longer pregnant. This meant that Rene visited me again for the following two months, shredding my body in his quest to procreate. He succeeded again.

"That time, I was leaving nothing to chance. Nan had disappeared after my fall, so I no longer had a confidante willing to help. I was on my own.

"I threw myself down the stairs a second time. I bumped my head and passed out. When I came to, I dragged my swollen body down to the kitchen and found matches. I did not care if I burned with the house. I wanted to die. I wanted to be sure to destroy the lives that burrowed inside of me.

"Once everything was engulfed in flames, I lay on the floor and allowed my spirit to escape my earthly bonds for what I planned to be a final time. I watched, detached, as Rene came riding up on a horse, truly embodying the fiend he was, screeching as he saw his legacy, his home, ablaze with the host for his monstrous offspring trapped inside. He burst into the house, his clothing already on fire, rushing from room to room.

"When he found my body in the foyer, he first checked on his progeny. A hoarse bellow of rage billowed from his chest. He picked up my body and walked towards the door. He took a step, and suddenly stopped. A mirror positioned by the door, where it shone directly in front of his face captured his gaze and he became as if paralyzed, and dropped me outside the door, onto the porch.

"I listened as he howled impotently, and the house began to fall down around him. I wavered in and out of consciousness. Blessedly, I do not know what happened after that point, because I succumbed to unconsciousness yet again."

She set her glass down on the table next to her and slid her gloves back onto her scarred hands.

"I thank you all for bidding me an audience. I had no one else in which to confide, as my parents died as soon as Rene took me from our townhome. I could not remain in New

Orleans after his death, so I will continue my journey. Maybe I will end up back there when everything dies down; maybe I will not. I wish you Godspeed in your adventures, as well."

She then spoke directly to me. "Perhaps you and I will meet again. I pray it is so."

Dominique walked, alone, to the stairway and left the club. None of us spoke after she left, out of reverence for the trust she had bestowed upon us. We never betrayed the confidence of another club member, and her secret would ride with our own to our graves.

The story should have ended there, but it did not. Try as I might, I could not keep Dominique from invading my thoughts. We had made a connection that night at the club. She haunted me and I would never rest until I had seen her again.

Years later, I travelled east to New Orleans to see if I could find any clues to where she might have gone. Inquiries on her name concluded with many widened stares, and more than a few crossings of the bodies and grasping of artifacts. I was finally led outside of town, to a burned structure.

Though few details remained, and the smoke had long burned away, my heart knew this to be Rene's original home. In the distance, another house peered through the trees. I rode in closer, following the sounds of children playing. My first glance of the yard's inhabitants was of four toddlers, sandy haired and dusky skinned, running around the side of the house.

Closer inspection revealed two servants, each rocking baby carriages made in fours in front of them, with bundles inside. One of the servants grasped her gris-gris in her hand as she performed her duties, fear etched on her face, arm extended as far as possible away from her body.

Standing on the furthest side of the house, I finally saw her, head tilted in the same way as she had held it that night. Her kinky curly hair was shorter than before, laying close to her head. She was still beautiful, from what I could see. I slowed my horse, still quite a distance away from her. She turned in profile, and I saw her extended belly, full of life. Even from my post several feet away, I could see frantic movement from within her stomach in varied directions.

She raised her gaze to look in my direction. I would have sworn I was too far away for her to see me, but her look was only for me. As she turned to more fully face me, I saw the exposed skull and tissue that should have been covered by skin. Skeletal hands and arms appeared from frock pockets. She moved in a stilted manner, haltingly, towards me. She raised one bony finger and pressed it to half lips, extending the kiss into the air between us. Dominique then raised her head towards the house.

In an upstairs window stood a man of dark visage, peering down onto the women and children in the yard. He then raised his head and looked towards the fields surrounding the house. I followed his attention. And there I found my true Dominique. She floated through the fields, unencumbered, untouchable.

Angela Eternal

The city art gallery buzzed with the excitement of its patrons. Awe filled squeals of delight could be heard exclaiming, "Oh, look at this one!" and, "Wow, this guy sure has a lot of talent." One of the most popular exhibits in the show was the one that showcased the work of a previously unknown artist, Taryn Slater. Her portrait, simply titled "Angela Eternal", drew the most public interest. Her reviews centered around the realistic nature of her paintings.

"I don't know, Harry. There's something funny about this painting," Myrtle uttered in a loud stage whisper to her husband. "I feel like…it's staring at me. That lady looks like she'll start speaking in a minute."

Harry grunted his disapproval. "A lot you know, Myrt. Don't you know all pictures do that; make you feel like they're following you?"

Myrtle was not convinced. "Okay, Harry, but this one is different, I tell you. Look at the chest. Doesn't it look like she's breathing? Pictures aren't supposed to do that." She continued her insistent pulling of his coat. Finally, she chirped with glee. "Since you know so much, tell me why the artist's self-portrait is so different from this one of this other lady, then. There's something missing. This one looks like a regular, flat picture. That other one looks...alive."

Harry sighed. "I'll never bring you to anything with so much culture again. Artists go through different stages with their work and..." he guided his disturbed wife away from the exhibit. A group of teen-aged boys had a different view of the artists' self-portrait.

"Boy, is she hot!" one of them stated emphatically, grabbing his crotch for the desired masculine effect.

The tallest member of the group shrugged uneasily. "I don't know, Bart. She ain't really all that."

Bart whooped. "She ain't all that? Man, look at that tight little body. And those lips...what I wouldn't give to get a taste of those."

"I think he's right, Bart. You have weird taste. She looks like a witch. A kinda pretty one, but still spooky." Their companion spoke up.

His observation of Taryn Slater was a commonly shared one. With sloped eyes the color of caramel, and a skin tone paler than paper, Taryn was not your conventional beauty. Her nose was too small for the generosity of her lips—and her facial structure so angular that skin appeared to stretch tightly over her bones. The self-portrait was very accurate, as she had taken no artistic liberties to create any other type of work other than a true painting of herself. Every detail was true—all the way down to the bluish aura surrounding her small, almost child like hands, lying daintily on top of her thighs.

"This has to be the tenth time I've passed this same clearing!" Angela Thomas banged her hand against the steering wheel. "I can't believe I'm lost. The owner said the cabins wouldn't be hard to find. I got the most detailed directions from her." Unbidden, tears came to her eyes. "It seems all I can do right nowadays is cry." She swiped angrily at the offending moisture. At the point that she realized that it was useless to try and stop them, she lay her head down on the steering wheel and sobbed openly.

Six months ago she'd visited Dr. Sherman's office. She and Zachary had been trying to have a baby for the past couple of years. Angela felt that her dedication to her career during most of the early part of their marriage had been one of the main reasons the union was now falling apart. A baby was definitely what they needed to get back on the right track with their relationship. When she missed her period, she didn't become too excited, because her periods had been rather irregular in the past. But when she felt the constant ache in her abdomen, she knew she would visit the doctor.

"So, Doc, when do I become a mommy?" Angela's heart beat frantically. Dr. Sherman turned concern filled eyes toward hers. "What's the matter, Doctor?" She placed her hands protectively over her abdomen, a habit she'd already fallen into. "Oh, don't tell me you saw more than one baby in there. I'm definitely leaving one of them at the hospital with you, if that's the case." She continued to caress her stomach and smile to herself.

"Angela, there are no babies." Dr. Sherman's voice sounded as old as his sixty-year-old body now looked, slumped over his desk.

"Wha..what?" Her face froze.

"There is no baby."

"But I feel it. My breasts are sore and I'm gaining weight. If there is no baby, then am I having one of those hysterical pregnancies, where I want so badly to have a baby that I'm making it all up?"

"I wish it were that simple. On the sonogram I detected an enlargement in your ovary. I suspect it's a tumor." Dr. Sherman took a deep breath. "It looks rather large, Angela. We'll have to do more tests to see exactly where we stand with this."

"Okay." Angela rose from the chair, numb. Dr. Sherman rushed to assist her from the office.

"Will you be okay, Angela? I'm sorry to have had to tell you this. Should I call Zach?"

"Okay." Angela allowed herself to be led back to the chair as Dr. Sherman tried to get in touch with her husband. Two hours later, after no word from Zachary, Angela finally convinced Dr. Sherman to let her drive herself home. She didn't hear from Zachary until the next morning, when he arrived home to find her still in her robe and not at work. "Where have you been?" she whispered half-heartedly. He didn't bother to answer. The lipstick on his clothes told her all she needed to know. She never wore that color.

Six months and numerous tests later found her on her way to the campsite in the woods. The cancer was too far gone, and chemotherapy was such a long shot that she opted to simply go in grace. She had enough saved to live on and the place in the ad she'd answered seemed the perfect place for peace. She almost hadn't seen it buried at the bottom of the paper in small print. And now she was lost.

She backed up the car and went once again to the main road. After deciding to go the way she'd first gone, she turned and drove around a raccoon in the middle of the dirt road. "There isn't anything I can do," she murmured to herself as she drove along. A few minutes later, she ended up back at the same road, but this time there was a woman bent over the raccoon. Angela was mesmerized as she watched the woman speak to the animal, in tones she could feel but could not hear. The woman then bent down and picked it up, holding it close to her body and stroking it almost sensuously. With each stroke, her hands seemed to be engulfed in a blue haze. Angela blinked furiously to clear her vision. The woman's eyes glowed also as she looked up and saw Angela watching. She came close to the car.

The woman smiled a sad smile. "You must be Angela Thomas." Angela drew in a deep breath.

"How did you know that?" She took another deep breath and held the gaze of the other woman.

"I don't get many visitors in this area. Besides, your accent gives you away. You sound like you're from upstate." The woman's strange, large eyes shined luminously from her pale face. "I am Taryn. I would shake your hand, but mine are both in use." Angela smiled back and looked at the raccoon in the woman's arms. The animal had stopped breathing. Suddenly overwhelmed by her own impending death, Angela felt her eyes fill with tears once again. She then shook her head angrily.

"I didn't see a car anywhere. Can I give you a lift?" she said through a water filled throat.

"We would like that." She unwrapped the skirt she was wearing and pulled it around the raccoon and placed it in the back seat. Then she floated to the passenger side of the car and slid in.

Angela was comforted by Taryn's mere presence. Her frustration at being lost in the woods faded away, and she felt the tears leave her insides. "I'm afraid you'll have to direct me because I've been lost out here for quite a while this afternoon." With direction from Taryn, she quickly found that she'd been in the right area the whole time. Taryn gave her directions to the cabin where she'd be staying and then issued an invitation for dinner. "I'll be there at eight," Angela assured her as she drove toward her own cabin.

By the time she'd unpacked, Angela realized it was almost eight o'clock. She walked in the direction where she'd dropped Taryn off and was pleased when she went right to the cabin. The door was ajar, and she knocked to announce herself. "Hello, Taryn. It's Angela. I'm coming in." She couldn't see the smaller woman anywhere in the main room of the cabin. As her eyes adjusted to the dimmer light, she found that the walls were covered with paintings of animals and plants. They were very good. Life-like. Then she heard a sound to her left.

Walking closer to where she heard the sound, she saw that in the corner sat a painting of a raccoon. Her heart began to race. The sounds were coming from the portrait. She realized that the sounds were coming from the squirming movements from within the canvas. Was that the same raccoon Taryn bought home earlier? Even closer inspection revealed that the slight movements were coming to an end, and Angela was compelled to touch the painting. As her fingers met the portrait, she felt the fur on the animal's back, and the movements of his tail as he regarded her curiously. Her fingers came away with blue tinged paint on them. She picked up the portrait and turned it over. The back was plain white and flat, as it should have been. But the front had a distinctive bulge, which although it was quickly melting into the flatness, it was still present. "How is that?" she mused. "I watched him die."

"I helped him." Taryn's voice came from behind her. Angela whirled around and faced the other woman. "He needed another home in another world, and I helped him." She strode to where Angela stood. "I help all the animals and plants here when they need to evolve."

Angela began to tremble. "You know I came here to die, don't you?"

"Yes. And I need to help you, too." She stretched her arms out toward Angela. Without any hesitation, Angela went to her.

"Will it hurt?"

"Not at all. And you will live forever." She enveloped Angela in the circle of her arms and began to stroke the taller woman until her hands and arms glowed blue. Soon, she had what she needed. Then she sat down to paint.

House of Haints

The little house needed as much rehabilitation as I. Its creaky steps echoed my broken heart. The open rooms paralleled my empty womb.

Steve took our much bigger house in the divorce, relishing in his ability to have my lawyer hand him the keys. I welcomed the chance to move away from the torment our marital home had become, even as I mourned the loss of what our life could have been.

Lost in the endless loop of our final day in court, I almost didn't see her face. The old woman stared at me, baleful, from the parlor window. I shaded my eyes from a non-existent sun, automatically assuming an illusion. I looked at the window again. Her dour expression, black frock, and bonnet faded before I could approach the porch.

I put my scant groceries in the kitchen and went to the parlor. There wasn't even a chair at the window the woman could have sat on. I was tired. Exhaustion and stress were horrific bedfellows. I hadn't eaten since the morning of the prior day. It was no surprise I was seeing things. I put together a quick dinner of cheese and crackers and headed to bed.

Sleep came, grudgingly allowing me a couple of hours respite from conscious existence. I never slept the whole night. That first night in my little house was no exception. That evening, singing, rather than anxiety, pulled me from slumber. The soul stirring melody beckoned me into the spare bedroom. A young woman stood in the middle of the room, her bare feet atop a crack in the hardwood I made a mental note to fix.

"Hello?"

The woman never acknowledged me. She continued to sing, fussing with her bags. She had several, bulky and unwieldy. Ragged. I tentatively walked towards her. Before I reached the spot where she stood, she disappeared. I backed out of the room, continuing to search for where she could have gone. I made it out to the kitchen and still didn't see her again.

Once I was awake, I was awake. I turned the burner on underneath my old teakettle and heated water for my favorite meal of late—a strong cup of tea. I unpacked dishes and waited for the water to boil. Soon, the wail of the teakettle broke my concentration. I reached for the pot but saw no smoke coming from its spout. The wailing continued, though I'd already turned the fire off.

The sound came from elsewhere in the kitchen. Movement caught my eye and I turned my head to see a little girl sitting in a corner. She screamed, writhing in a growing puddle of what looked like blood. I ran to her, tears burning my eyes. Her mouth formed a perfect "O" and I reached for her, encountering only icy air before her screams abruptly cut off.

I was again alone in the room.

Shaken, I discarded the notion of tea. I returned to my bedroom and searched for the white sage I'd planned to brush the house with when I regained my energy. I had no one to call. I couldn't just pack up and leave. I had nowhere to go. The only money I'd gotten from the divorce was tied up in the house. I had to rescue myself from the apparitions in my new home.

I fumbled with the matches in the pouch alongside the herbs. Misty swirls floated into the room, forming into the two women and the little girl. I felt no fear. Only sadness. The little girl's pain was my own, radiating through my womb as I relived my own abuse. I leaned against the bed, tired from my own baggage, heavier than that of the young woman. Weariness permeated my soul as I felt the despair of the older woman, her sadness a reflection of my own.

I put the sage and matches away. They belonged in the little house as much as I did. I could not exorcise the haints any more than I could exorcise my own soul. We all would haunt together.

We would rehabilitate each other, in our little house of haints.

Mama's Babies

When the dog jetted out between my legs as I opened the door, I knew Ray hadn't let him out that morning.

Figured.

Three kids and fifteen years later and Ray still threw tantrums when I left the house alone. If that was the only time he acted a monkey, I'd be home free, because I rarely ever left the house without him or the kids. Unfortunately, that was only one thing that would set him to pouting.

I used to think those full lips were the sexiest thing ever, even in the childish pout. But everything got old after a while when it was tied to a one trick pony.

I glanced out the kitchen window to make sure Woof hadn't gone too far towards the river. He was nowhere to be found. I briefly debated going to find him, but I needed to check on the girls. If Ray hadn't let the dog go poop, he likely hadn't changed Evaline's diaper, either. I knew it was getting harder to get her out of her wheelchair to do that as she got older, but it had to be done.

A quick look at the kitchen counter told me he hadn't fed the kids, either.

Figured.

I was only gone for three hours that morning. The trip from Richmond into the outskirts of Houston took a long while, but I took extra time to relish my temporary freedom from doctors, whining husbands, and three little kids who needed me so desperately. I didn't mind the kids needing me. That's what Mamas were for. But Evaline's special needs were getting hard to juggle with a four and seven-year-old to bounce on my hip, too. And Ray adding to the burden and not to the help.

I wouldn't have had to go find a pharmacy in the city that morning if he'd just done it on his way home from work the day before. The girls came home from school with some kind of virus, and it made their eyes look funny, like bleeding tears. Janey said she felt sick and I could only imagine that Evaline would have said the same thing if she could talk. I pleaded with Ray to go to the pharmacy right then, to see if he could get some ointment or something for their eyes, until he got paid again and I could take them to the doctor.

"I only get off work one day a week early, and I'm not wasting my time going to no damned pharmacy. They'll be fine. You baby them too much."

"Really, Ray? Look at them. You're not worried about this? They don't look good."

"They'll be fine. I'm going to the café to hang out tonight."

I smelled expensive cologne on him and knew he was probably lying. If he left, I couldn't even load up the kids and go to the pharmacy myself. "The café doesn't open until nine. It's only four now."

"I got stuff to do, Zenobia. Get off my back about it." He left, slamming the screen door behind him.

I turned to my babies, lined up in the kitchen behind me, Evaline moaning more incessantly than usual. "Okay, Mama's babies, let's go put in a movie. Ray Jr., it's your turn to pick." My sweet-faced baby boy smiled at me with uncharacteristically tired eyes and ran into the living room. I unlocked her wheelchair and followed Janey to the couch.

Two movies later, Evaline and Janey were burning with fever. I though Ray Jr. felt warm, too, so I gave them all fever reducer before putting them to bed a little earlier than usual. After my shower, I sat in bed with a book, too preoccupied to really read it. Instead, I stood and went to the bedroom window. The room overlooked the back yard, which bordered the Brazos River.

I hated that old stinky river, hated the river critters even more. I was glad to only have to chase two kids out to the fence. Janey and Ray Jr. always wanted to take Evaline with them on adventures, and I was glad her wheelchair made them move too slowly to get completely away from me. They loved their sissy and I knew they'd take care of her when I passed on. We really couldn't count on their daddy to do much of anything.

After I finally fell asleep, Evaline cried out loudly. I stumbled into the girls' room. Her bed was full of diluted blood, still leaking from her eyes. The fever seemed to be breaking, but she thrashed around like she had severe gas pains. Janey tossed in her little bed, too, but she seemed to stay asleep. I changed Evaline's sheets and rocked her until she calmed. Then I lay her back down and pulled up the bed guard. Ray Jr. slept peacefully in his room

I didn't go back to sleep that night. It looked like I might have to take Evaline to the emergency room in Rosenberg if the bleeding didn't stop. I called Ray's cell phone and got his voice mail. He never did answer or return my calls, but finally showed up at the house at seven the next morning.

"I'm taking the girls to the ER."

"No, you ain't. We don't have money for that."

"They're still sick. I have to try and get them to see a doctor or get some medicine or something."

He ignored me and walked up the stairs. I followed him.

"Ray, none of us hardly slept last night."

He went into the girls' room, at least having the decency to move quietly. He peered through Evaline's bed guard. "She's sleeping fine now." He looked at Janey's bed. "Her, too."

I didn't believe him, so I went to check my babies myself. They were sleeping peacefully, and their brown, smooth skin was cool to the touch. Really, really, cool. The blood streaked tears had stopped, too, dried remnants pooled on the towels I'd placed underneath their heads.

"I still need to get some medicine. And since you clearly hadn't planned on going to work today, you can stay with the kids while I drive into Houston. The girls can't go to school like this." When he didn't have a ready retort, I knew he was hung over and had had such a busy night that he simply didn't have the energy to fight or argue with me.

I dressed in a hurry and made one last check in the kids' rooms. They hated for me to leave them behind, and I wanted to be gone and well on my way back before they were up for too long. I hated to be without them, too, but the walls of the house were closing in on me. We only had one vehicle and I was the one who was left without, day in and day out. The kids and I entertained each other well enough, but sometimes I wanted to be around other adults. Besides, with the girls gone to school all day, Ray Jr. and I were left to play with Woof. In the fall, my baby boy would be gone to school, too, and I'd be left with only the dog all day.

I drove below the speed limit to extend the drive. On a whim, I stepped into a coffee shop before sincerely looking for a drugstore. I never felt more like a fish out of water than when the young barista complimented me on my locks and all I could do was stare at him, open mouthed. He was probably my age, and wasn't asking me to marry him, or even go out on a date. I mumbled my thanks and escaped back to the truck with the coffee, my freedom now sullied. I had to get back home to my babies.

The pharmacist wasn't familiar with any of the symptoms I described in my girls, so she suggested I bring them in to the onsite clinic they had. I told her I would, but that I wanted to make them comfortable first. I knew I wouldn't be able to bring them. I think she knew that, too. She kindly pointed me towards an eye ointment on the shelf and an additional fever reducer to alternate with the acetaminophen I was already giving them. I thanked her. For a brief moment, I was jealous of her, getting to spend hours on a job that paid her for her time.

I drove home just above the speed limit.

Forgetting Woof, I walked slowly up the stairs. My brain struggled to decipher the sounds I was hearing, like the dog had found something to put in his mouth and chew and suck on that he wasn't supposed to have. But it couldn't be Woof. He'd abandoned me.

The door to the girls' room was ajar, as usual. I could see the bottom wheel of Evaline's overturned wheelchair and I ran to the room. My heart pounded in my throat as I expected to find her or Janey trapped in or underneath the heavy chair that weighed more than each of them. The girls weren't under or in the chair. They were on the floor, next to their father.

Janey clawed into Ray's stomach, tiny purple hands scooping entrails to her small mouth. She slurped, like Woof with forbidden contraband. Evaline lay on her stomach, scooting close into Ray's neck, her limited head movement not hindering her meal of his throat cartilage. She'd never eaten anything orally, since birth, only fed with a g-tube. Now she chewed and smacked and gobbled.

My bowels tightened. *My babies.* I backed away from the door slowly, towards Ray Jr.'s room. My baby boy wasn't there. I checked in my bedroom, keeping watch on the girls' room at the end of the hall. I ran down the stairs, two at a time. Ray Jr. met me in the living room. Blood streamed from his eyes.

"Mommy, I don't feel good." *My babies.* His fat cheeks glistened with blood and pus. Dark purple bruising settled around one side of his face. I reached to pick him up, wanting to run, wanting to scream. But I only had a little time before he'd turn like the girls.

Instead, I ran my hand lovingly across his tight curls. "Mommy needs to go get some more medicine. And maybe some ice cream." My voice cracked and I couldn't breathe around the lump in my throat.

"Okay. Then I'll feel better?" He stepped closer to me and licked his lips.

"Yes, baby. Why don't you go into the living room and watch a movie?"

"Okay, Mommy." His short legs moved in a slow amble, in stark contrast to how he'd gone into the same room just yesterday.

I ran out to the yard and into the truck. I'd left they keys in the house, upstairs in the girls' room. I threw myself out the truck door and headed for the woods along the river. I jumped the fence and stumbled over Woof's body, his fur crusted with blood. He paddled his legs fruitlessly, and I kept running.

Freedom.

Bushes cut my legs and face as I tore through them, trying not to look back at the house.

Escape.

Trying not to look back at the house where my whole life was.

My babies.

I stumbled to a stop against a tree. I continued to run. Back home.

I pushed the door open and Ray Jr. stood in the kitchen, waiting for me.

"Mommy." He reached up with pudgy arms, for his Mama.

I lifted my baby boy into my arms and hugged him close to my heart. He nuzzled his wet, baby face into my neck. He would turn, like the girls, soon enough. Maybe his sisters would make it down the stairs by then, Janey helping Evaline drag along, down each step.

Conflict Resolution

I t couldn't have been trying to hide, the way it poured from the brush and lay on the side of the open road.

"What the fuck is that?" Brandon squinted and leaned closer to the dashboard. "Didja see that?"

I had seen the flurry of movement in the outer circle of the van's headlights. The tall brush moved violently, as if something huge slid through it.

Granted, it was dark, the kind of dark that only seems to happen on lonely Texas backroads. Brandon and I drove slowly down the rocky path, trying to prolong our limited time together. We turned a sharp corner and there it lay.

The headlights didn't reflect off its eyes the way they did with most animals. We almost missed it, in fact, because there was no reflection.

"What's that?" I asked.

"What *is* that?" We both questioned, words exploding simultaneously. We laughed. Even though we'd only been together a short time, it seemed we thought with one brain, we were so close.

Now, we'd had some beer at the drive-in theater. We liked to go there to see our movies because we could bring our own food and weed. And we could fool around in the back of Brandon's old van. They always showed two movies, so we had about four hours to do the things my mama wouldn't let us do at other times. But we weren't drunk.

Brandon backed the van up, slowly, turning slightly so the headlights shone in the direction where we'd seen the thing.

I don't think either of us was ready when the lights found their target. Reclined in front of us was the biggest piece of roadkill I'd ever seen. Longer than I was tall, with two human-looking legs.

The legs were attached to a chewed-up torso, also humanlike, but with no skin. The flesh was mangled, but not oozing like I would have expected.

Impossibly long arms, strewn out in front of the thing, like human bones that also served as chew toys. I felt Brandon looking at me for an answer, but I was mesmerized by our discovery.

"What could possibly have chewed on it like that?" He turned wide eyes back to the road.

"What is it, even?" I whispered my question.

Looking at the head made things worse. I felt the beer bubble up in my belly and threaten to spew as my stare landed on a desiccated deer head, antlers and all. Then the thing moved.

"It's still alive." Brandon put the van in park and placed his hand on the door handle. "We have to try to help it."

I grabbed him, pulling him closer to me. "Do you see that thing? It has no skin on most of its body. We can't help it. It's gonna die anyway."

"You're right. But we can't just leave it." Brandon was really sweet like that sometimes. It was just like him to want to help a monster.

I sighed. "Okay. Let's leave it some food. That seems like a merciful thing to do. At least it won't die of starvation before its injuries kill it."

Brandon left the van running and grabbed the leftover snacks we had inside. Then we slowly walked toward the thing on the ground. It didn't lift its head, but it began to clench and unclench its massive fists, which were tipped with what looked like talons. It hadn't looked that large in the headlights. The beams didn't cover the creature's full length. It was easily eight feet tall.

I was glad the thing was injured. The sharp teeth jutting unevenly from the mouth could have easily torn us apart.

Brandon put his arm in front of me to keep me from going too close. He must have also seen that the thing was larger than we'd originally thought. Its hands, if outstretched, might have reached us.

In his free hand, Brandon held the bag with the hot dogs and chips we'd nibbled on earlier. He gently tossed the food toward the creature, near the clenching hands. We stood back and watched it for a moment. It continued to stare at us, its mouth hanging open, the lolling tongue laying between the many teeth.

Suddenly, a clenching hand grabbed the bag. The thing played with the food for a few seconds, before trying to half throw and half shovel it toward its head. The movement created a moist, sucking sound, as exposed tendons and muscle worked against one another.

I again felt the urge to throw up. "Maybe we should cover it up, too. Buzzards will be here soon and pick it apart before it even dies."

Brandon pulled me toward the van as the creature finally got some food near its mouth. The long, mottled tongue snaked out and dragged the remnants into the mouth. I jumped into the van, too horrified to look away but too frozen to help, as Brandon tossed a sheet over the lower half of the creature.

"Let's go," I mumbled to Brandon, who still stood outside the van. I reached to honk the horn just as he turned back toward the van. All I'd wanted to do was enjoy the feel of the smooth, slick leather on my skin where it peeked out from beneath my miniskirt and maybe play around some more on the way home since everything was still tingly from earlier. Maybe smoke another joint or pop another X. Now, I didn't want anything other than to leave the monster where it was and get away.

Brandon finally got back inside and put the van into gear. We started to drive off, with him hitting the brakes once to take the next turn back out. The faint red of the brake lights illuminated the thing in the rearview mirror. Its head was raised, eyes following us out of the area.

Brandon pulled the van up, half a block from the fourplex where I lived with my mother.

"Damn. You know Mama'll be tripping again since it's ten minutes past midnight." I hated hearing my mother's mouth about every little thing. I hated my mother. She still gave me a midnight curfew at the age of twenty-two. It didn't matter that I had a job and went to college full time. I was almost done with my degree and she still treated me like a child.

"I wish your mama would get a life. Find a man. Or a woman. Something so she can leave us alone and get out of our business." Brandon didn't like Mama, either, and that was okay, too. She didn't like anyone anyway.

"I wish she would just fucking disappear." I gave him a lingering kiss to keep myself on his mind through the next couple of days. "Text me when you get home. If I don't answer back, it's because she took my phone." I slid from the van and walked the rest of the way to the apartment.

The slap caught me unawares, even though I shouldn't have been surprised.

"The hell you been, you little tramp?" Mama was on a bender. I smelled her before I felt the backhand. She hit me again, this time punching me in the chest. The wind spurted out of me and I doubled over. The drugs I'd had earlier helped take the edge off the pain. But the drugs Mama did around the clock made her especially strong.

"You'll get enough of dealing with that little nothing-ass boy. He don't mean you no good. Get your dirty ass in your room. And leave that damned phone out here."

I struggled to catch my breath. "No."

Her eyes widened and she took a lumbering step closer to me. "What you say?"

I stood up, still gasping. "I said 'No.' I'm grown. I pay most of the bills here. You can't tell me what to do."

She snatched my hair up in her hand and twisted it tightly. I tried to lean into her grasp as I felt some of my tracks slipping. "Oh, you got you a little piece and now you smelling your ass. I'm still the mama." She punched me in the face. "And you gonna respect me." She punched me again, this time in the eye. I saw blinding stars across my field of vision. She reached back to hit me again.

"I wish you were dead!" I yelled at her. "I wish you were fucking dead! I'm sick of you fighting on me. You didn't care about my dirty ass when you were tricking me out to your boyfriends, so don't worry about it now!"

Our neighbors wouldn't hear me. They were either out partying or strung out. They never heard when Mama beat me and threw things at me. If they did hear, they wouldn't care. They never came to help or call the police or anything. I was on my own. Like always.

Suddenly, Mama let go of my hair. I had been leaning against her hand, and I fell backward from the momentum of my weight. Mama hung from a long, cadaverous arm, high off the ground. My brain refused to comprehend exactly how much strength it would have taken for anyone to have lifted her that way.

But the thing was super-strong. It shook Mama like a rag doll. It clenched her from the back , its talons protruding from the front of her large body . I hadn't remembered them being that long. The creature took a swift bite and half Mama's head disappeared. I watched as the skinned ribcage expanded with the bounty, then flattened again.

It ate at her again and again until nothing was left and hardly any blood spilled. My eyes met its gaze. An unspoken message passed between us. I had called. It answered. And then it was gone.

I should have been in shock, but I called Brandon. "You have to come get me."

"Why? You okay? Your mama fighting you again?" I could hear the squeal of his tires.

When he arrived, I was waiting for him at the corner. I shivered, the realization of what had happened finally weighing on me. I told him the whole story.

Brandon pulled over to the side of the road and stopped the van. "You're sure it was the thing we saw? It was dying. How do you know it wasn't another one?"

"*Another one?* We don't even know what this one is, much less if there're more somewhere. I just know. Its eyes were exactly the same. It was different, though. Stronger. Fuller. Juicier." I shuddered as I remembered the teeth.

"And it just . . . ate your mama? Like, all of her?"

"All of her. Real fast."

"And it didn't hurt you?"
"No, it didn't want to hurt me." I struggled to find the words to say what nagged at me. "It's almost like I wished Mama dead and it came to help me."

Brandon whooped until tears cascaded from his eyes. "You mean like a zombie genie? Granting wishes and shit?"

"Either a genie or a golem. Either way, it sort of spoke to me inside my head and told me that."

Brandon continued to laugh, but started to drive again. "Shit, if it's granting wishes and shit, then wish for 4 million dollars and seventeen cents." He continued to guffaw. "Matter of fact, I wish it would eat my damned boss so I don't have to go to work tomorrow." He grew solemn and squeezed my knee. "You've never spent the night with me and I want to stay wrapped up in you all night and all day long."

We got back to his apartment, where Brandon made good on the first half of his desires and I stayed the night. Exhausted, I decided I would cut classes the next day and just head in to work later that night. Early the next morning, Brandon's cell phone rang.

As he answered with one-word responses, his brown face grew ashen. He ended the call and stuttered. "I . . . I don't have work today. Mr. Teeter, he . . . he was murdered in the shop last night. It'll be closed until they finish the investigation."

We stared at each other until he began to jump up and down in the bed. "It worked! That shit worked!"

I felt queasy about our good fortune coming at the expense of others' lives, but then I thought about how many times Mr. Teeter had messed up our plans and underpaid Brandon for all the overtime he worked, and I smiled. I didn't know that old man. And Mama had deserved every bit of what she got. I moved back into Brandon's arms to make good on the second part of his wishes.

We spent the rest of the afternoon thinking of everyone who had ever done us wrong. "Remember that damned bully I told you about from fifth grade?" Brandon asked me over hot wings.

"Yeah. He sounded like the worst."

"He was. I hope he dies a horrible death."

"And my microbiology professor. She's a stone-cold bitch. She needs to be erased." We fell into a fit of giggles, sharing ranch dressing–laced, weed-high kisses.

Over the next few days, I stayed with Brandon and continued my regular routine. The news channels reported a serial killer that was especially vicious. They also reported on numerous unexplained disappearances. The police had no leads and the town was in a panic. No one would probably miss Mama until her dope boy came ready to deliver again. The investigators would eventually see the connection between all our victims. We needed a plan to leave town.

We took some time to research our creature. Its description fit that of a wendigo, an immortal creature that ate human flesh. They usually didn't venture to warm locales, though, so we were stumped as to how it had gotten all the way down to Texas. But we really didn't care what had brought it to us, global warming or whatever. We were just glad it was clearing our lives of haters.

Brandon and I watched just to see who caught it next. Our zombie genie was coming through for us in big ways. All our death wishes were granted swiftly. We quickly figured out that we had to kill off Brandon's relatives who could leave him money, and that would be how we'd get rich and bail to Mexico.

One night, Brandon's phone rang while he was in the shower. I picked it up because there was no caller identification on the screen. "Hello?" I answered the call, thinking it was the shop calling Brandon back to work.

"Ummm . . . is Brandon there?" It was a woman.

"What do you want with him?"

"He's the father of my kids and the one I'm carrying now and I don't owe you any explanation anyway. Who the hell are you and why're you answering his damned phone?"

I saw red. I hung up the phone and burst into the bathroom.

"Why the fuck didn't you tell me you got a baby mama tucked away somewhere?" I snatched the shower curtain so hard the rod fell on Brandon.

"Wait. I can explain." He slid around in the tub trying to evade my slaps. "I wanted to tell you. She wouldn't let me go."

"How pregnant is the bitch now?" I continued to slap and punch his wet body.

"Four months. But wait! Angel . . ."

"Wait, nothing. We been together for seven months. You been seeing her all this time? Since before me? I'm the fucking *other woman*?" The hurt I'd been trying to ignore stabbed through me like a blade. I collapsed against the bathroom wall.

Brandon struggled to wrap a towel around his body, still explaining. "We were on a break and she was sweating me about getting married and shit. I ain't ready for all that. Then she threatened to go get my child support increased if I didn't stay with her. I had to try and pacify her on that."

"So you pacified her right into another baby? Okay."

"Angel, baby, please. I love you. I don't love her. She's trying to make life hard for me. For us. Just let me get her off my ass so we can be together." He wrapped me in his arms and I could sense his hesitation. He wanted to know if I was buying it.

"So you're leaving her to be with me?"

"Yeah, baby. Yeah."

I stepped back just far enough so he could see my face clearly. "She's the enemy, then?"

"She is, baby. It's just you and me in this. Forever."

"Then I wish that bitch was dead. And those damned babies. All. Of. Them."

Brandon's mouth formed a perfect circle as my words registered. He scrambled to get dressed. While he did, I threw his van keys out the window as far as I could.

"Go on and run to your bitch, now. How fast can you get there?" I pulled on my clothes, determined that he wouldn't leave me behind if he managed to find the keys.

The joke was on me. Baby mama lived only a few blocks away. I followed behind Brandon as he raced into one side of a small duplex, wrestling with a key I didn't realize wasn't on his key ring.

By the time I got through the still-open door, Brandon was cradling a woman in his arms. She was half-eaten, the bottom half of her body gone, ripped apart directly beneath her belly, where a piece of the recently detached umbilical cord lay on the floor. Chewing noises drew my attention to the corner of the room where our creature stood, a tiny leg hanging from between his jaws for a brief moment before he swallowed it, too.

Brandon never looked at the creature. He caressed the woman's face, kissing her and mumbling, "I'm so sorry. I love you. I'll always love you. I'm so sorry."

His words hurt more than I thought possible. I was beyond hurt.

"You can go join her. I wish you were gone. I can't stand to look at you anymore."

The words had barely fallen from my lips when our creature moved from the corner. Slobber dripped from its jaws as it stood above Brandon. He didn't have time to yell before it bit his shoulder.

"No! No! I wish you would eat her. Eat Angel."

I couldn't believe he had the nerve.

The creature turned toward me, dropping Brandon. It seemed hesitant and I moved in quickly. It served both of us, so I had to eliminate the other master.

"Eat Brandon quickly, starting with his head. I wish he didn't have any more time to speak." The wendigo turned and devoured my ex-boyfriend where he sat on the floor with his lover. It also completed its abandoned meal, and so both traitors were gone. I watched, partly in awe, partly in satisfaction. I slid across the room and sat down at the dining room table to think.

The creature followed me there. I wanted to ask why it was sticking around that time, but before I could do so, it grabbed me in its talons and pressed the deer mouth into mine. My lungs filled with rot and decay. I felt my body dying as the beast continued to breathe more and more deeply into my essence.

As I filled and grew and transformed, its voice spoke inside my head. "Accept me. Your spirit is soiled, more so than his.I will live in you, the blacker of the two souls."

It became me and I disappeared.

Flesh of My Flesh

I breathe their sweet scents, sighing at their freshness. My babies are cuddled up next to me, one on each side, and I twist my neck to plant kisses on their smooth chubby faces. A police siren threatens their slumber, and as the wail grows louder and then trails off, I am the one who needs comfort. I rub my daughter's knee, relatively unlined, and devoid of the darker, tougher skin that develops as one ages and uses the joints—for kneeling. Begging. Crawling.

My own knees carry the same calluses and scars that can be found over my entire body. The C-section scar from the deliveries, an assault that still feels numb in places and itches all around. I also have the usual childhood scrapes with sharp objects, and the remnants of my war-torn heart. It's also numb in places. My throat, where my last lover left his vicious mark, feels everything.

My son sighs in his sleep and screws up his face at a nightmare. I see his fears as vividly as if they are my own. I nestle him closer and stroke his stomach until he soothes. His nightmares will never cease. His brown body will be subjected to living monsters seeking his blood and the vestiges of his soul. My daughter will fare no better. I will raise her to be strong but she will be beaten back until she is incapable of aspiring to any better than we have now.

I will do anything for my babies. I press another kiss to soft, kinky curly haired heads, and feel the blood pulsing through their tiny temples.

I keep vigil at night to keep the rats from feasting on my precious darlings. I brush roaches from their pajamas and hum to cover up the sounds of the neighbors fighting long into the darkness. My need for food and rest vanished in the wake of making sure they had enough of both. I wished my need for companionship had also vanished.

The loneliness led me to him. I was an easy mark: a single mother with no high school education, existing in the ghetto I called home. He said he loved me. I pretended to believe him and gave him my body. He took my entire being.

A thin trickle of sweat begins at my daughter's crown and makes its way down the side of her face. I bend slightly and lick it off, closing my eyes at the delight her innocence brings.

He did me a favor. He left me, battered and bleeding. But I became stronger as I recovered. And I understood that my experience had allowed me the means to get my babies out of this hell. When the time came, I would deliver them, much as I had two years ago. I allowed myself another taste.

Flesh of my flesh. I will deliver them to a more bearable hell.

Bad Feet

Minerva Pitts had an old lady name and old lady bad feet. She wasn't worried about the name. Nicknames helped. Besides, she was a middle-aged woman who often got pegged at fifteen years younger than her actual forty-five years.

But them feet.

For as long as she could remember, Minerva's feet had done their own thing. Her father still regaled her with tales of how they could never find shoes she'd keep on when she was a little kid and how even when they thought they'd won the battle, they'd find she and her feet had dispensed with one or both of the shoes they thought would last. Shoes just never lasted for her. Quite a few things didn't last for her.

It wasn't that her feet were extraordinarily big or small or fat or skinny. Her feet just hated to be cooped up inside shoes all day, every day. She could usually manage, on good days, a few hours a day with shoes on. After that, they were dispensed of, sometimes nicely, sometimes, not so nicely.

Her memories were dotted with shoes ripped to shreds or simply disappeared into where ever missing shoes went. She'd put them on and as long as she stayed happy, her feet stayed happy. After too long, neither she nor her bad feet were happy being cooped up inside for hours and hours and the shoes had to go. She could usually tell when her feet were about to dispense of shoes not so nicely. She learned to remove them so they wouldn't be destroyed. Trying to keep from getting angry or wanting to remove people who weren't treating her nicely before her bad feet could kick in was a whole other thing.

Minerva was homeschooled throughout her childhood. She loved being home with Mama while Daddy was at work and she learned so much. Mama often took her for long walks through the woods so she and her feet could run through the foliage and climb the trees. Besides, there was something about a shoeless little girl that most school administrators just weren't feeling.

"It's okay, Mama's Baby," her mother had cooed. "You're just too special for them."

She'd taught herself to dance as a toddler and her parents had even allowed her to enroll in a modern dance class across town when they saw her skills. The teacher complimented her every class session. "Minerva, you dance like an angel." "Dearest, never stop dancing." Minerva hardly wanted anything as much as she wanted to dance. Her feet had to dance and frolic to all the music. Sometimes, to no music at all.

But when Ms. Michelle begged Mama and Daddy to allow Minerva to study ballet under her, too, they refused. "We can't afford the shoes," Daddy claimed. He lowered his eyes and glanced at Mama.

The way he and Mama looked at each other told Minerva they were lying. "Daddy, it's not nice to..." she started, but Mama shushed her.

She could also tell that Ms. Michelle knew her parents were lying but couldn't do anything about it. Minerva quizzed them when they left and got back in the car.

"Why did you tell that lie, Daddy? Mama, you said we should never tell lies and you let Daddy tell a great big one. Why can't I go learn different dance with Ms. Michelle?"

Minerva remembered the look of Daddy's eyes in the rear-view mirror. She had never wanted anything more than she wanted to dance. In that moment, it was all she could focus on. It was what she and her feet wanted most in the whole world and Mama and Daddy were being mean to them all.

"You know you got bad feet, Baby Girl. Just enjoy the modern classes with no shoes. All the other types of dance require keeping shoes on for a long time and that won't be good for your feet."

Minerva was so angry, she thought she would pop. "But dancing makes me happy. It makes my feet happy! We don't care if we have to wear shoes to do it sometimes." Her six-year-old self didn't understand the concept of controlling emotions and she began to cry and kick in the backseat. Through the fog of her anger, she could hear her parents calling to her to calm down and watch them feet.

Minerva kicked and screamed until the car came to a sudden, jarring stop. She continued to thrash until Mama and Daddy circled her in their arms as they stood outside their car. The vehicle looked like it had been wrecked from the inside out. The front of the vehicle tilted in a crumpled heap at the foot of the light pole where it had landed, not quite touching the pole, but rather, resting against it. Holes the size of bowling balls dotted the doors. The roof was blown off. The front seats were smashed against the dashboard and a large piece of fabric torn from Mama's dress hung from the jagged frame outlining the missing roof, marking their escape route. The back windows where Minerva was sitting were all broken out, one with the shattered glass still hanging in the frame, a single hole punched through.

She stared up at her parents. The unconditional love they typically displayed disappeared, exposing something different. Fear. Even as a young child, Minerva instantly understood her parents had always held back this scary emotion up to that point. Her tantrum terrified them. Minerva wanted to make them happy again. So, she danced. She and her bad feet pranced and leapt and spun until their fear was covered with the resolute silence they mostly masked themselves with.

They walked home, Minerva insisting she wanted to walk all the way on her bad feet and her parents on each side of her, walking in silence. She felt bad that the condition of their car was because of her. But she and her feet were walking…and dancing! So, she was happy and so were her bad feet.

However, Minerva never asked to take any other dance classes again and quit modern dance just before she turned fourteen.

When it came time for her to go to high school, her parents finally gave in to her numerous pleas to be allowed to experience social events like other kids her age. Minerva had her heart set on dancing on the school drill team. She couldn't do that from home. She wanted to look at the audience as she danced and danced. Minerva really looked forward to the way the drill team dancers danced in the stands every time the band played a song. She hoped their band would never stop playing music so she and her feet could dance every Friday night through the football and basketball seasons.

She couldn't dance on the team as a freshman, so during that first year of high school, she struggled to keep her shoes on all day and sat in the back of the classrooms so she could take the shoes off while she worked in class. She was really good at making people forget she was sitting right next to them, so no one caught her during those first months. She wanted to make sure her grades and conduct marks stayed high so she wouldn't be barred by the administrators, or her parents, from auditioning at the end of that long year.

Minerva aced the auditions with a contemporary routine she choreographed herself. During her interview, the director complimented her effusively.

"I've never seen such technique. We just may have to get you to help the captain with some routines this year. You might even make captain someday…soon." Minerva felt the side-eyes many of the team members gave her. She ignored them. All she wanted to do was dance.

Mama and Daddy questioned her about the drill team summer camp. "How long will it be?" "How far away is it?" "You will watch them bad feet, won't you?" She'd never been allowed to go away from home with her parents, not even to relatives' homes. Her being separated from them was new for everyone and she felt a little sad that she wanted to be on her own for a few days.

Minerva thought they worried too much. She shooed them away when they dropped her off at the campsite. "I'll be fine. And I'll watch my feet."

She skipped into the main building to get her room assignment. The only thing that could have possibly made her any happier was if they'd started teaching the camp dances on the spot at registration. She knew the instruction would start soon enough and the thought helped her calm her feet. First, she had to get settled into her cabin. Her feet moved to their own beat as she made her bed and put away her things. Happy, bad feet.

Her happiness lasted only as long as that night. After a vigorous short routine, Minerva felt her face heat up as instructor after instructor gave her kind words about her movement. Several of the girls joined in, gathering around her. She mostly noticed those from her own team who didn't join in. In fact, the anger swarming off the captain of her school's team, Lainey, burned Minerva down to the soles of her bad feet.

Lainey cornered her in her room while Minerva's three roommates were conspicuously absent. "Don't get to thinking you're hot shit, Nerve. I'm the captain of this team. And you, you're nothing but a darkie dark nappy headed big lipped wanna be. Go back to Africa."

Minerva's first instinct was to laugh. Lainey was black, too, although she had a much lighter complexion than Minerva's smooth dark coloring. Lainey wasn't an ugly girl, but she acted ugly. Mama had always told her that you could be as pretty on the outside as you wanted to be but if you were ugly on the inside, then it would make you ugly all the way around. That was the way Lainey looked to her. A twinge of pity began inside Minerva when she tried to understand that people like Lainey only had one thing going for them and they felt threatened when that one thing might be taken from them. Everybody couldn't be like her and have two wonderful feet that would always be with them and keep them happy.

Then she noted the ugly nickname Lainey had called her and the pity vanished. "Hey…"

Lainey pushed her down against the small wooden dresser. Minerva fell onto the floor, bottom first. "Take your ugly ass back to wherever you came from, Black Nerve."

Minerva was so hurt and angry she thought she would pop. Negative feelings swirled inside her until she felt a sweet release. She had, indeed, popped. Her feet grew and grew until swirling, shimmering brown tentacles swarmed from her soles. Fluorescent colors shone through, the appendages waving in the dim cabin light, dancing to a beat only they and Minerva could hear.

Lainey stood, mouth open, rooted to the floor in the middle of the room. The tentacles wrapped around the girl, squeezing until her face darkened, though still not as dark as Minerva. Rows and rows of exposed teeth glimmered in the light the appendages created. Still, they danced, holding Lainey as an unwilling partner in their waltz.

Tiny nibbles at the girl's body turned into all out voracious devouring. They chomped and slurped and lapped at the blood and gore covering the hardwood floors of the cabin. All that was left of Lainey when they were done was her team spirit hair bow. Minerva had one already, but she figured two wouldn't hurt. She waited until the tentacles had all slid back underneath her skin, returning to her feet, before she retrieved the bow. Her feet felt happy. Not bad at all. She felt happy, too.

After the incident was investigated and it was determined that Lainey must have simply run away while at camp, the drill team director held a special try out for an assistant captain. The previous assistant captain inherited the top spot that Lainey had vacated. Minerva had easily won the second in command spot. For a brief moment, she contemplated going for the captain position, but decided it would be too risky. Besides, she hadn't yet understood how to control them bad feet of hers.

Throughout the following years, she honed her skills and studied what made her feet do the most terribly beyond bad things. The happy emotions kept the monsters at bay. The negative ones triggered their appearance. And only when Minerva really, really wanted something. She spent her life not wanting much, finding complete joy in dancing and teaching dance to children. Her feet made her happy and kept her young.

I Want to Be Free

I always thought I was just a chick with severe daddy issues who always chose the wrong men, but, no: there was something trying to kill me.

I first saw it when I was about five years old, when my father had his hands around my mother's throat, choking her. This was his regular thing to do, get drunk and then take out whatever perceived slights he'd received from the world on us. At that time, Mama bore the brunt of his abuse. He didn't hit us when we were little. Instead, he just ignored us, like the little unwanted kids we were.

That night, my little sister and brother had already gone to sleep and I was up, alone, terrified that would be the night he would finally kill our beloved Mama. I peeked from around our bedroom door, gaze fixated on my parents in the dining room of our small fourplex apartment. The floor plan was a straight shot, reminiscent of the shotgun houses in other parts of the city. I had a clear view of the two of them tussling, Mama trying to pry his hands from around her neck and him just as determined to keep her in his grasp until…

I knew to be quiet, no matter how scared I was. The last time I'd cried out, he'd kicked Mama, hard, just to show her what he would've done to me if I was older. She whimpered but endured the onslaught, because she didn't want him to turn his attention to me. It was hard to stay silent but I couldn't bear to allow her to die without knowing I loved her enough to witness her death.

Mama knew I was there because our eyes met briefly while he had her pinned down, backwards, on the dining table. He hardly ever paid us any attention, so I didn't think he knew I was there. His face, contorted with sweaty rage, remained focused on his task at hand.

Tears streamed down my face and I watched Mama grow weaker, struggling to catch a breath. Suddenly, a different face from his turned towards me. Enlarged eyes buried underneath a ledge-like unibrow, and elongated teeth jutting from between thick, dried out lips. The monster hardly had a nose, instead, two nostrils sat in the middle of its face. I shook my head to rid myself of the vision. My father couldn't have been looking at me. He was still focused on my mother, lying prone beneath him.

It wasn't my father. And it sneered at me, mouthing, "You're next."

I blinked my eyes rapidly, petrified with fear. Mama finally pried his hands from around her neck and he stumbled backwards, his drunkenness putting a stop to his attack. She gulped in heavy breaths and looked at me to let me know she was okay.

I ran back to bed and pulled the covers up over my head, happy she was still alive. Terrified that I had seen a monster more terrifying than my father.

By the time I was a teenager, my father's amnesty from his beatings had long worn off. He still targeted Mama and never attacked my sister or brother, but I had become his favorite punching bag. One day when I was sixteen, and before I left for drill team practice, he called me a bitch and I wasn't in the mood for his shit.

"I'm not a bitch. You're a bitch. You're the one laying up here with no job and fighting on your wife and kid because you're a weak little bitch."

I figured if I was going to get hit, I'd get some hits of my own in with the best weapons I had: truth and my words. On cue, he flew up from the sofa where he'd taken up long-term residence and came running at me. I couldn't completely escape him in our tiny apartment but I usually had a tiny bit of room to negotiate how I'd defend myself.

All thoughts of defense left my head when I saw the closed fist coming towards my face. It was larger than my father's hands, by at least three times. I stood, in awe, at how I could see the shadow fist extended over his flesh one, all at once encompassing it and allowing it to move at the same time.

My awe cost me valuable seconds of maneuvering and I caught the fist right on the side of my head. Stunned, I realized I'd taken the blow from the shadow fist. I scrambled blindly across the floor, keeping my eyes on the everchanging form of my father, which had morphed from the mean-spirited and abusive man I'd known all my life to the same creature I'd seen years ago. The same bulging eyes held me in their gaze. I could still see my father's eyes and twisted expression but the face superimposed over his held my attention.

I couldn't hear what my father was saying as he caught up to me where I lay in the floor and wrapped his hands around my throat. He jacked me up against the wall and I marveled at how the huge shadow hands held me fast against the sheetrock. They pressed and pressed against my throat, jutting brow almost meeting mine. I could see the saliva drip from the teeth, worried about what it would smell and feel like if it hit my drill team practice uniform.

The face then started to laugh in my blurred vision, cackling its victory as I began to lose consciousness.

From somewhere behind my father, Mama appeared, as a dream-like overcast figure. She held a frying pan which she brought down hard on his head. My father winced and turned to face her. I was still briefly held up against the wall by the shadow hands. Neither of my parents noticed. I gained a second wind and began to kick furiously against its strength. The face stopped laughing and the hands began to disappear. One of the eyes winked at me, its parting shot unheard by my still ringing ears but clearly understood by my blurred eyes and head: *Next time.*

"Leave my baby alone!" Mama shouted. "You're always beating on me but you're gonna stop beating on my child." She brandished the frying pan in front of her like it was a gun. I coughed furiously and moved away from the both of them. That was the first time Mama had ever come to either of our defense and the shift in dynamics was palpable.

My father slinked away back to his couch and Mama took me into the bathroom to help mitigate my injuries before my friends came to pick me up for practice. I could tell she wanted to ask me not to go to practice because everyone would see that I'd clearly been beaten. She didn't ask, though. She silently applied cold water to the growing knot on my head as tears rolled down her face.

I wanted to ask her about the monster I'd seen. Had she seen it, too? But the sorrow and guilt in her gaze stopped me.

Instead, I reassured her, "I'll already be home from practice by the time the bruising on my throat starts to show and I can wear a headband pulled low over the knot." I wasn't sure I was right about the bruising, but I hoped having dark skin would help in the situation.

My friends still saw it all when they arrived to pick me up and gave me silent space to work myself into my drill team captain persona. They gave me sympathetic looks and hugs of solidarity and I wanted to tell them about the monster, too. I couldn't.

After that, Mama's newfound courage kept my father from putting his hands on either of us ever again. But the monster still made his appearance. Sometimes it would appear on my father's face as he slept, its eyes open wide, watching me. Other times, it appeared when my father verbally abused us, smiling when the human man was scowling and calling us names; moving its arms and legs in my direction as my father remained rooted in his couch. It taunted me, showing up when I least expected it, promising unspeakable consequences for me.

I had to leave home.

I graduated from high school with a pocket full of scholarships and a few items of clothing that I packed up to take to my dorm. I spent as little time as I could at home during that first year of college, even though I attended a local university close enough that I could walk back to my childhood home. I had to return briefly, with my tail tucked between my legs, when the scholarships ran out and I couldn't afford to stay on campus any longer. During that brief return, I never looked at my father and walked around him like was a piece of furniture. I could feel the monster's gaze, even though I would never meet it. I wasn't sure how long I would have to avoid them both until I could get out on my own.

When I finally moved into my own tiny efficiency apartment a few months later, I breathed a sigh of relief. I never had to go back home if I didn't want to. I could always visit with Mama and my sister and brother when they came down to road to my apartment. I was finally safe from my father and the monster.

My high school sweetheart and I had broken up so I dated occasionally. I sought out men who were nothing like my father. They were tall where he was short. They were mostly silent where he was always talking. They were less bookish than he was and they gravitated more towards athletic endeavors and rap music.

During this time, I dated a police academy student. He assured me that he wanted to be a policeman so he could help our community. I went to his apartment with him one night after we came from the movies. I couldn't really make up my mind if I wanted to sleep with him or not but the decision was made when he came up behind me and wrapped his arms around my waist, kissing me softly on my neck. I fell into his tenderness and allowed him to lead me to his bed.

Soft and gentle remained until the moment he entered my body. I flinched, eyes flying open to confront him for not having taken his time with me in that entry. His solemn face had been replaced by that of the monster, smirking as the flesh moved within me roughly. I tried to push him off me but was unable to raise my hands from the bed. The large shadow hands held my arms fast to the mattress, pressing my wrists down into the softness.

I whimpered and the flesh moved faster, harder. Pounding into my body with each movement marked by searing pain. The thick dry lips grazed the side of my face, laughing when I tried to turn my head away. Saliva dripped down from the fangs, mingling with the sweat our human bodies produced. I cried and stopped moving, deciding the best way to get through was to just endure. At the human moment of orgasm, the monster threw back its head and howled, a haunting sound I heard in my soul, blood turning to ice at hearing how much it enjoyed torturing and hurting me.

The flesh man suddenly wiped at my tears, jumping away from me. "Are you okay?"

I scrambled across the bed and sat on the floor next to it, trembling while I tried to find my clothes.

I followed his gaze to the bed where streaks of blood lay garishly against his sky-blue sheets. His eyes widened.

"I'm so sorry! Did I hurt you? I'm sorry!" He moved towards me, genuinely remorseful at the scene unfolded in front of us.

I backed away, still crying. "I just want to go home."

He took me home, attempting to apologize a few times before I cut him off. "I know you didn't mean to hurt me."

Next, I dated a boxer who wanted to show off his moves to me one night after we ate dinner in his gym. The monster appeared and knocked me onto the floor of the ring. The flesh fist had been nowhere near my shoulder but the shadow fist made up the distance and floored me.

I went out with a dentist who rolled his car over my foot. Large hands and snarling face superimposing his while he rummaged in the glove compartment for something. He thought he had accidentally taken his foot off the brake, but I knew better.

The couple of months I spent with a realtor ended when a pipe he was standing next to but hadn't touched fell and hit me across the back when we were visiting a home he was representing. I stepped out of its path just far enough so the blow wasn't as disastrous as it could have been…far enough that I saw the huge, hairy thigh that had pushed the pipe down.

Apparently, I just couldn't date anyone.

I reunited with my high school sweetheart. A man of few words, he was the opposite of everything from my father and the other men I had gone out with. I didn't count him as out of bounds because I knew that man like I knew the back of my hand. We had matured quite a bit since high school and the worst thing I had to worry about with him was the cheating. I'd hoped he was beyond all that once we got back together. For a while, we were happy. We had a baby boy and moved in together. The future looked pretty bright.

It was a false front.

The last big fight we had started because I saw all the calls he'd made to a woman in another town while I stayed in the hospital with our son during an asthma attack. He lied about the woman, even when the evidence was in front of his face. I yelled at him that I was done and he needed to get his stuff and leave the apartment where I paid the rent and the bulk of the bills. I had no sooner issued the command when he stalked to where I stood in our living room.

The calm natured boy grown into a calm natured man wore the distorted face of the monster that had haunted me my whole life. The muscled chest twice the size of the flesh heaved with unbridled anger. Fangs stuck out beneath snarled lips. Large eyes narrowed at me, and veins appeared on the thick neck that was larger than my whole head.

I screamed when the flesh hand reached out to grab my arm and the shadow hands reached me first. Pain laced its way up through my upper arms where I was held captive. The hands squeezed; the snarling morphed into laughter around the concerned flesh face.

"...I just want to talk to you. We can work this out." Genuine confusion danced across his face, especially when he looked down to where he held my arms and witnessed the bruising that had already started. "I—I wasn't grabbing you. I didn't mean to hurt you."

I barely heard him as I quietly repeated my request that he just leave the apartment. I rubbed my arms, crying, knowing we could never work out. Not because he was a serial cheater or we weren't really all that good for each other, but because the monster would never leave once he'd appeared.

For much of my son's childhood I didn't have time to date and I was fine with that. Until the friend of a friend started expressing interest. I wanted to ignore him but my heart and body wanted something different. I fell head over heels when I overhead him tell my son, "I want to be your step-daddy one day."

We moved cautiously, living together for a couple of years before venturing into marriage. I didn't like everything I saw. He was quick to anger, although he never turned it on my son. He was overly jealous and controlling and while I thought it was cute at first, it got old really fast. By the time he proposed. I didn't know how to turn him down. I wasn't ready to confront the downslide I was sure was ahead of us.

So, I accepted and we got married.

Where I'd thought he was controlling and jealous before, he became downright abusive after we married. I got pregnant quickly with three more kids, spaced only a year and a half or so apart. Staying pregnant through those early years of our marriage is likely what saved me from escalating abuse. He never shoved or hit me while I was pregnant. But after baby number three between us, I didn't have the protection of pregnancy anymore.

One night, I woke up with half my head in his mouth. I felt the heat of his teeth, boring into my skin like knives, threatening to take off my whole cheek back to my neck. I cried out in pain and leapt off the bed when he released his hold on me. In the glimmering moonlight creeping through the curtains, I saw the glint of sharp fangs, working to regain their assault on my flesh. The thick lips surrounding them smacked and worked, trying to free themselves from the flesh. I yelled at my husband to wake up, to stop the attack, sure he would rather hit me than bite me. The shadow face scowled as my husband shook his head to rid himself of sleep and it.

"What's wrong? Why did you wake me up?" He turned on the nightstand light. His eyes widened when he saw the slow trickle of blood on my face. "What happened to you?"

"You bit me." I knew he didn't care that I was hurt. He would only care that I had marks I could report.

"I didn't bite you. I mean, I was sleep. Maybe I was dreaming…I didn't mean to bite you." He pouted like a child being accused of something he was reasonably sure he hadn't done but couldn't deny completely because of past behavior.

I went into the bathroom to clean the wounds. He went back to sleep.

The monster had found me, yet again, and this wasn't just a man I was dating or living with. He wasn't my father, whom I'd been able to finally escape. I was married to this host. I was a full-time homemaker with no job prospects and I had four children to take care of. If I stayed, it would kill me if my husband didn't. But how could I leave?

My husband found increasingly more compelling reasons to stay away from home. He claimed to work long hours and professed a need to stay at work overnight on some nights. I knew he wasn't working all that time but I was grateful for the respite. Whenever he was home, the monster resumed stalking me, watching me from the corners of its eyes, taunting me. Threatening me. Promising my destruction. I just needed time to finish my degree so I could take care of myself and my children.

I just had to meet my goal.

My husband had been cutting off my avenues for freedom throughout the years. He wiped out our bank account each week, leaving barely enough money for me to pay some of the bills. He commandeered my car and took it to work himself, leaving the children and me at home without a vehicle for long days at a time, even though he had another vehicle that he parked somewhere other than our house.

I made plans to take the kids out for the day and told him that we would take him to work so I could have the car. He exploded and knocked the car keys from my hands.

"No, you're not."

I had grown so accustomed to his abuse that I momentarily forgot to check and see if it was him or the monster threatening me.

Before I could respond, he had me in a chokehold against the floor, hot breath raking across the side of my face. He sat on my body and I could see the shadow torso sitting upright on top of me, hairy chest heaving. The bulging forearm pressed against my throat also partially covered my mouth. There was no flesh man on top of me. Only the shadow monster, empowered by the constant rage my husband had built up towards me.

Muscled, hairy thighs held my lower body in place as he raised his free hand to turn my head in the opposite direction, a move that would break my neck. Dry lips cracked and bled in its glee at finally having me helpless in its grip. Spittle ran freely from its fangs and pooled on my blouse. My vision began clouding and I couldn't fight any more.

"Get off Mama!" The high-pitched voice came from up the stairs where my babies were. I could see the outlines of their little faces pressed into the spaces between the bannister poles. The monster finally took its attention off me. And looked directly at my fierce little daughter. It grinned.

I couldn't allow him to curse her the way he had cursed me with his presence for a lifetime. I found a reserve of strength I didn't know I had and bucked underneath him while he was distracted. I unseated him for a quick second and then rolled my body to a prone position where I could bend my knees and force him off me.

I struggled to take in air and charged him with everything I had left in me. I slammed him against the hall table and picked up the decorative bowl on the table and crashed it against his head. The monster fell to the floor, fading back into my soon to be ex-husband.

I ran upstairs and gathered my babies. We went into a bedroom where I called the police. The officer came and took our statements. I listened to my husband lie about the events, not caring. We both ended up with domestic assault charges. I endured the court meetings and the ensuing divorce battle where my husband's lawyer argued that he shouldn't have to pay me anything for spousal support because I was violent towards him.

I just wanted to be free.

After the divorce, I never dated again. I didn't need to fill that void in my life and my children and I had a good life. I found a job I enjoyed and took pleasure in watching my children grow into teenagers. I'd probably feel the despair of an empty nest much more than other parents did, but I'd make it through.

The other day, I turned to my son to tease him about having outgrown his third pair of shoes for the year. Out of the corner of my eye, I saw the glint of familiar fangs and a hint of nose holes above thick lips, superimposed on my sweet baby boy's face. I swung my head fully towards him and the image disappeared.

I just wanted to be free.

I Get Mad, Too, Sometimes

So much craziness happens in my 'hood. It isn't strange to see folks doing things that might seem out of place in other parts of town. I mean, I was half walking and half running from the bus stop, dressed in uniform and struggling to remove it to reveal the street clothes I had on underneath. That was crazy in itself, so when I saw the brother on his knees next to the bayou, I slowed my pace but kept walking.

"Evening." He never turned to acknowledge my greeting. I slowed a little more, transfixed by the way he dug at the earthy-smelling mud with his bare hands, muttering.

"She's so mad. I have to find them. She'll never leave me alone about it. Gotta hear her damned mouth forever and ever." He recited these words over and over, a sad song harshened by the rough edges of anger.

"Lose something?" I came to a complete stop at that.

"I have to find them. Tired of hearing her mouth. I get mad, too, sometimes." The man never turned to face me, but he did answer. "Wedding rings. I tossed our wedding rings here on the side of the bayou. They didn't go in, but I can't find them. I get mad, too, sometimes."

I'd have been mad, too, if I were his wife. How dare he throw wedding jewelry away? I wasn't sure how to answer, though, so I simply continued my trek home along the bayou. The body of water stunk all to be damned but cutting through the bank was the quickest way home. Speaking of hearing nagging mouths, I hoped my sister didn't have any words that day when I arrived. She had to keep my kids while I worked my second job and she thought that help entitled her to talk smack about everything, all the time.

I turned the bend in the waterway and focused on the sun, still high in the sky at four something in the evening. It was always so hot in July. Seemed the sun never really set before it was up again, blazing through another summer day. Something glittery caught my eye.

There were all kinds of things in that bayou, but every now and then, there was treasure to be had. I chastised myself for wishful thinking, but still, my feet found their way to the part of the mud closest to the water. Laying just beneath the surface, sitting on top of the concrete embankment, was a glint of gold. Rings, to be exact. I turned to look around. The man who was on his marital jewelry hunt was well behind me, far around the corner. I slowly walked towards the rings to get a closer look.

Two gold rings lay in the water, barely covered by the muddy liquid. The only reason I saw them was because they looked almost like they'd been placed just inside the water line. I looked around again. Surely the man wasn't playing a trick on me, planting his jewelry some unsuspecting bystander would find them and pick them up. My heart quickened. *That was dumb.* And if he was still behind me looking, that probably meant he didn't know where they were. *Who's to say these are his, anyway?*

I could really use the money. The diamond on the lady's ring alone would bring some good hard cash from the pawn shop. I could pay a real babysitter and tell my sister to go back to her own house. The man's ring also had diamonds, but likely wouldn't bring much from those stingy crooks at the PayWay Pawn. *He's already in trouble, anyway. I bet he can buy another set for him and his wife.*

I looked around one last time and flicked the rings from the water and into the mud. Casually, I bent down and picked them up. I was surprised at their weight. I placed them in my pocket, mud and all, forgetting all about arriving home in clean clothes that didn't reek. I didn't mind stinking for a cause.

Irma met me on the porch of my little row house. "Let me tell you what your bad ass kids did today…" She went in and I just didn't want to hear it.

"Irma, please. I'm tired. I just worked 17 hours straight. Can I at least pee before you start?" My newfound fortune made me fly at the mouth.

Irma looked at me like an actual fly had caught her in the mouth, but she didn't say anything else. Three of my four little ones came running from the back bedroom they all shared. "Mommy, Mommy!" The cacophony of their chirps made me want to scream. Instead, I blew them kisses and ran to the bathroom and shut the door behind me. I locked it behind me. Closed doors meant nothing to them. Or Irma.

I sat on the closed toilet seat and turned on the water at the faucet. I cringed when I thought about the increase in the water bill, but decided it was worth it to get just a few minutes of peace and quiet. Life wasn't supposed to be the way mine had turned out, but it was what it was. When you shacked up with a man who said, "Baby, just let me finish my law degree and then we'll be set," but you didn't get that shit in writing, or get around to doing any legal documentation, you got what you got. What I got was four babies and abandoned. Javon used that law degree to divorce me and leave me and the kids with bare minimum. I had to work two jobs just to try and make ends meet. The ends got further and further away, though.

I pulled the rings from my pocket and slid a towel across the sink drain. I rinsed the rings and examined them more closely. The center diamond was larger than I'd originally thought. The facets glittered as I turned it underneath my dimming bathroom light. I didn't know a lot about diamonds, but my gut told me that one was real. The band clearly matched the ring, but it was also clear that the masculine counterpart was an afterthought. The solitaire ring was the most important part of the duo.

I'd never had a wedding set. Javon said it would have to wait until we were settled and he started working in a firm. I used to wear a cheap, sterling silver placeholder ring so I could pretend the father of my children loved me enough to marry me. It made my finger itch and I threw it out after a few months.

I slid the solitaire onto my wedding ring finger and followed it with the band. I held the rings up to admire how they shone. I thought maybe I had them backwards, but it was all just for pretend, anyway. As much as I hated the judgment that came with being an unmarried mother, I couldn't afford to let my pride cost me the pawn money the rings would bring.

Banging at the door made me jump, and the band slipped off my finger and onto the towel in the basin. I pulled at the solitaire, trying to get it off, too.

"What?" I swear I couldn't even find peace in the bathroom.

'You have a visitor." Irma's voice travelled through the door, unusually subdued. I couldn't imagine who it could be to get her to shut her mouth like that. We rarely had visitors, unless it was her husband coming to fetch her home when he thought she'd been there too long with us. Even then, I suspect he only came because she called him to rescue her.

"Just a minute." I tugged at the ring again, still unable to get it off. I turned the sink off and scooped up the band. I put it, and my left hand, in my pocket. I ran from the bathroom.

I walked into the front room and watched as a portly, seasoned woman played hand games with the kids, all four of whom were transfixed on her movements.

"Hello." I spoke, almost not wanting to disturb them. My kids were never quiet, not even in their sleep. My baby girl went and sat in the woman's lap. The other three followed to stand around them.

The woman smiled at me. "The babies. Beautiful." Her voice barely registered in the small room. Her mouth barely moved. I wondered if it had moved at all.

Irma grabbed my arm. "Who is this woman?" Her grip faltered. She was shaking.

"I don't know. I was looking for a sitter. Maybe someone from work had an auntie…"

The shaking turned into barely restrained fury. "A babysitter? Oh, and you weren't gonna tell me? How you think you gonna pay this babysitter? I keep your hellcats for free and you suddenly come up with money to pay somebody else?" She snatched at my arm until my hidden hand came free of my pocket. Irma's eyes turned to slits. "Oh, it's like that? When were you gonna tell me something?"

"Irma, I..." I get mad, too, sometimes. I wanted to tell her off, to cuss her out—something. But the hurt in her eyes as she snatched around gathering her stuff had me momentarily silent.

I felt more than hurt coming off the woman sitting on the couch. I thought I momentarily felt pure fury mixed with anguish anchoring me to the floor. Her stare fixated on the ring I was wearing. I had to be confused with the energy Irma was putting off. Flustered, I put my hand behind my back and watched Irma storm away from the house. She was really pissed because she marched, straight backed, in the direction opposite from where she lived. I guessed she would meet Ray on the way. *Nah, she's stubborn enough to walk all the way home just to spite me and make me feel bad.*

The negativity left with my older sister. A glow of comfort washed over me. Whoever the woman was, I really needed her to babysit. Irma wouldn't talk to me again for weeks and I had to go to work. And the kids loved the lady. I remember Mama always telling us that little children had built in bullshit and danger detectors. If someone wasn't right, the babies would know. Besides, if something jumped off, I could take her.

"Did you hear about the job from Maisy at the Steak and Shake?" I had only told a few co-workers about my problem. Maisy was the most likely to really try to send someone who would be reliable enough to come.

The woman tilted her head to the side. "The babies. Beautiful."

"I know it's last minute, and I promise we don't always have this kind of drama here. When can you start?"

My oldest son looked up at me, tears in his eyes. "Do we have to stop playing now, Mommy? We want to play some more."

I stared into his pudgy face and sighed. "How do you feel about a trial run while I take a bath? I'll pay you for the hour." The woman smiled at me and continued her game with the kids.

After the drama with Irma, a bath sounded like a welcome respite. I ran the water and tried to remove the ring once again before finally giving up and stepped in. Suddenly, I was frozen in the tub, unable to move. The ring tightened around my finger and black edges appeared around my line of sight. Images of a couple fighting filled my head. Angry words tossed back and forth. Dishes thrown. A knife pulled. Tearful begging. The man didn't want to die. The woman wanted to kill him. She would kill him.

Water, sloshing all around, sucking at my body. Earth-scented mud surrounded me, filling my mouth and my ears. I flailed, trying to get up. The gritty sludge made its way down my throat, into my lungs.

I sprang up, clawing at my left hand. My finger swelled, bursting over the edges of the ring. My entire arm ached, and I tried to rub some relief into it. I couldn't remember having left the tub and gone to bed. I walked as quickly as my aching body would allow and stumbled into the kids' room. They were still asleep. I made my way into the bathroom where a glance in the mirror brought forth a gasp. I looked like hell warmed over. My face was bloated and I had bags underneath my eyes, for the first time in my life.

Numerous bruises appeared all across my neck and upper chest, a difficult feat with my dark skin. I tried to wash my face and bring back some semblance of personhood. It didn't work. I looked at the wall clock. I was running late for work. Just as I contemplated risking being fired by calling in, the front door opened and the woman walked inside, going straight to the kids' bedroom.

"Good morning. Thank you for coming back. Can we talk about your pay when I get back this evening? It should be around five." I didn't wait for a response. The sitter was in and as bad as I felt, I needed my job. I got dressed and headed towards the bus stop. I'd get into major trouble for being late, but at least I would show up. I needed to get to the pawn shop first, though, to see if they would be able to get the ring off my finger. I didn't want to damage it, but I needed it off.

I walked the long city blocks towards PayWay Pawn. A hand squeezed my shoulder. I spun around and faced the man from the day before at the bayou.

I looked at him in the full morning sun. The glisten of madness shone from his face. "She finally shut up. I slept.

She stopped fussing. I can live again. I didn't have to die with her."

He shook me so hard my teeth rattled. When his gaze landed on the ring I wore, he shuddered. "No. That's done. I get angry sometimes, too. No." I watched as the man backed into the oncoming Metro bus. The bus wasn't going very fast, but it couldn't avoid crushing the man. I didn't have time to be horrified at his death. I ran back towards my house.

I opened the front door, calling for my babies. Water sloshed throughout the hallway. I slid in the puddle and fell, scooting towards the sound of running water. The ring on my finger tightened and ribbons of blood mingled with the water on the floor around me. I half slid and half scooted to the bathroom door.

The woman sat on the edge of the bathtub and held two of my children, one under each arm, their limp bodies dangling, twisted hair dripping onto the floor. The bathtub water ran on and on. A small hand slid over the rim with the water sloshing out. Lifeless. On the other side, a tiny leg bumped her ample hips as the body it was attached to threatened to slide out onto the floor. The woman faced me, fury roiling from her and heating everything in its path. "I get mad, too, sometimes."

I Will Only Love You
Better After Death

I loved her; in ways I had just begun to love myself. Wholeheartedly. Without hesitation or reservation. Absent of judgement and shame—with my whole soul.

The first time she smiled at me I thought I would surely explode at the way her warmth ran through me. She was a big, beautiful, sturdy girl and I never tired of watching the way her dark, muscled arms rippled in the scorching sun as she chopped away at the weeds in the plantation yard. Massa put her to hard physical work like the men folk were doing.

On the list of things I hated him and his family for, this was at the top. Deecy was too gentle for that abuse. Her fine, plump hands should've been, at the very least, tending to young ones in our quarters.

She never would have been in the house learning sideways how to be a lady from tending to the ladies of the house; her skin was too dark for that. Yet, she deserved to be a lady, more so than those afforded that title. She should have been surrounded by finery, eating the remnants of delicious foods, and relaxing in decadent baths that someone else drew and tended for her.

She should have been pampered. I wanted more than anything to be her servant in that way.

"Tell me again how much you love me, Ru," she implored, skirt splayed out around her on the ground in our special clearing where we sneaked to hide away from everyone and everything else. That big, grassy circle in the woods was the closest we could ever come to a place of our own. We found it and claimed it, marking it as ours with our love.

I quoted Elizabeth Barrett Browning's Sonnet 43, the first poem I'd learned to read because my first master's daughter, Emily, fell in love with a different man every week and walked around reciting the sonnet while I tended to her. "I love thee with the breath, Smiles, tears, of all my life; and, if God choose, I shall but love thee better after death."

Both Deecy and I could read well. She just loved the affectation I added to the words, a remnant from my life before that plantation. I had been groomed to be a lady's servant and gifted to Emily in the big house on the property where I was born. My slight frame and dusky complexion marked me acceptable for the task even while my aversion to wearing dresses and petticoats did not exclude me.

I enjoyed learning to read on those breezy afternoons when I stood fanning Emily in her bedroom, the window open and allowing more sounds than cooling inside. She spoke each word carefully, waiting patiently for me to repeat after her. As she sounded out the markings, she also traced the letters with her fingers, showing me how they worked together to produce the magic of sentences, paragraphs, and stories.

I even enjoyed well enough the stolen kisses and caresses Emily imparted on me when night fell and we were to be asleep. She only instigated those gentle explorations when she was between suitors but I welcomed them, nonetheless. The fumbling molestations I escaped from the boys on the property were infrequent because I despised them and made diligent efforts to never subject myself to their handling.

My duties did not take me outside the house and when theirs brought them inside, I hid behind my mistress until they left. She allowed me to do so when she fully understood I did not feel anything of a sensual nature for the boys.

I was not supposed to sleep in her quarters with her but she begged her father until tears shone in her eyes and she bit her heart shaped lips until they bled. He acquiesced, as he always did where she was concerned. Night after night, she taught me a new way for us to please one another and gave me the opportunity to practice my lessons.

I could not say I loved her so much as I was fascinated by the variety of sensations we could elicit from one another. I enjoyed her female body and with her, I could accept my own—even if only grudgingly and in the dark cover of night.

Emily's ploys to manipulate her father were not successful the night he followed her mother into Emily's bedroom and they caught the two of us entangled in her bedsheets, bodies pressed fervently together. By the time we were alerted of their presence by her mother's loud, scandalized gasp, it was too late to recover.

My old master yanked me by the hair and dragged me from her room. I spent that night on the porch, still naked, after he called me every revolting thing he could think of.

"You're not worthy to sleep with the other slaves because you're a lowly thing beneath even those cursed beings."

I dared not argue with him or defend myself. My naked female body held me in agreement with him, the form that had momentarily brought me pleasure with Emily returned to my source of enduring shame.

The next morning, he threw a ragged shirt and a pair of pants at me and watched as I put them on. He never removed his gaze from my naked body, shaking his head and whispering what a waste I was. He muttered variations of this exclamation throughout our wagon ride into town. Before the morning was over, I found myself sold to a plantation owner who lived two towns over.

My new master allowed me to continue wearing pants. He also gave me one admonishment: If I did not learn to do field work to his satisfaction and make the yield of three slaves, he would breed me out with his male slaves to make up the difference in inventory.

That threat of forced mating was all the impetus I required to get caught up to speed with the other field hands. Within a few months, I had learned to use my slight frame to the best advantage and could pick faster than all but two of my fellow field slaves.

He had not known what to do with me as far as sleeping quarters went. "I can't put you with the girls because you need to leave them alone and let them breed. I can't put you with the boys because you ain't a boy. I guess that means you bunk with old Odessa."

That was how I came to reside with the plantation's root woman, Odessa. The master did not call her a root woman. He called her a midwife. I did not know if that was because he was unaware of the totality of her skills and knowledge or if he simply disregarded them. I did not disregard anything about Odessa. It would have been not only disrespectful but unwise for me to do so.

On the first night I was deposited onto her porch, she looked me up and down and opened the door to allow me to enter.

"What's your name?" She spat a pungent stream of tobacco tainted spittle into a metal cup.

"Ruth."

"Mmmhmm. But what do you want to name yourself?"

I slowly looked up at her, the first time I had ever met the eyes of an elder. Her wizened orbs saw through me. She saw past my outward presentation and felt my spirit.

"I can name myself?" The thought was preposterous. I had never considered such out loud to anyone else.

"You can. The name they give you don't match you. Don't match your true self." She spat again. "What do you want to name yourself?

With my brain fogged over in possibilities, I uttered the name I called myself inside my head. "I like Ru."

Her wrinkled face split into a wide, toothless grin. "Then Ru you are. Come on, Ru. Let's make you a bed."

There was no magical epiphany wherein I suddenly felt free. How could I truly be autonomous when only one of the ties binding me had been loosed?

Nonetheless, by the time Deecy came to the homestead, I was completely Ru, fully vested in a personhood that could then at least dream of true freedom.

I introduced myself as such when she stumbled into the field, viciously prodded by the master's eldest son, David.

"Get your barren ass out in the field with the other menfolk." He shoved her one last time and left her, fallen, in the dirt close to us. I and one of the men ran to help her up.

She straightened her skirts and faced me. "What they call you?"

"I'm Ru."

"I'm called Deecy. How about you show me what I got to do out here, Ru?" Despite her previous abuse, she smiled at me.

I would never dream of anything but her.

A few weeks later, I was awakened from such a dream by light tapping at the cabin window. I was unable to remove myself completely from the bonds of slumber to investigate before Odessa spoke quietly.

"She came after you because she sweet on you, too. Go visit with her for a spell."

Odessa's ways were no longer surprising to me. I accepted that she knew things none of the rest of us did and I did not question how or why. I observed her whenever I could and she trusted me to help her sometimes. I simply did as she instructed.

When I finally faced Deecy underneath the full moon, she grabbed my hand.

"Come on, sleepy head. I got something to show you." Her whispered words fluttered over my head and caressed my ears. I would do anything she asked.

Odessa's cabin lay at the edge of the woods so she could easily gather the herbs she needed. It did not take long for Deecy to lead me to a clearing deeper inside the foliage than I had ever explored.

"Ain't it beautiful?" Deecy exclaimed, as soon as we were too far away from the cabins and big house for anyone to hear or see us. She spun around in a circle, bathed in the soft light of the moon. My breath caught in my chest as I watched her, wishing she could always be this free, that we could taste freedom together. I allowed her to spin me, too, until we collapsed onto each other amidst the grass blades, in a fit of giggles and drunken, heady exhilaration.

I rolled towards her and caressed her face. "You are beautiful." I kissed her, unable to remember the lessons Emily had taught me. I did not need to be taught how to love Deecy by anyone other than herself.

She was an eager teacher and I, her eager pupil.

Our clearing became our home, the place where we spun dreams and loved each other as freely as we possibly could. Every time we could get away unseen, we ran away to our natural "home".

"Do you think we'll ever be free?" Deecy asked one night as we languished in the aftermath of our lovemaking.

"I hope so. I want to marry you. Build a life with you. Maybe try farming."

"I love the trees here. Can we have lots and lots of trees on our farm?"

"We can have anything you want, my beloved." Even the empty promises felt good to make. I wanted Deecy to be happy.

We both knew we could never be married as long as we were enslaved on the plantation. Massa would never allow it because no additional inventory could be produced from our union. And although Deecy could not be bred because of a childhood injury that had left her unable to have children, I still lived under his looming threat to breed me.

She grabbed my hand. "I would love that."

Raucous laughter and yelling startled us. We had never encountered other people that deeply into the woods so we suspected a large animal. Deecy picked up a large stick and I wrapped my hands around two large rocks.

What emerged from the woods was entirely animalistic but human.

"See? I told y'all they was going to be here." David led a group of his brothers and friends towards us. "I seen them run out here the other night."

They surrounded us and began to grab and attack us. Deecy and I were outnumbered, two to eight. We had no chance of beating them away but we would not consider giving in without all the fight we had.

Soon, I was imprisoned by five of them who held and punched me. Deecy lay prone on the ground with the other three holding her.

"Since you wanna play with sticks and need to know what a real man feels like anyway, how you like a taste of this?" One of the men defiled her with one of the large sticks. Her pain pierced my soul and I fought harder.

One of our captors punched me in the stomach so hard I could not catch my breath for long moments.

"Don't hit that one in the stomach. We gotta show her she ain't no man like she thinks she is. Pa ain't gonna appreciate it if we make her barren, too."

"Well this one ain't having no babies anyway so we can do what we want with her."

They abused my beloved Deecy over and over again until her precious blood spilled over our clearing. I cursed them the entire time, until my voice diminished to a rasp. I held her gaze and watched the light slowly leave her eyes. The more they dimmed, the more empowered I felt. She had long ago given me her heart and body. She was then giving me her soul.

I had watched Odessa perform lifegiving rituals numerous times for sickly infants and the other slaves she healed. I knew all the words and ancestors to call upon. She had often warned me against using the opposite of these incantations to do harm to others, lest I bring the same harm back to myself.

She had never said anything about me not doing the harming, myself.

I used the part of her being Deecy had given me to call upon the entities who would avenge us, trading our lives for the power of vengeance.

The men stopped their assault on Deecy, who was then unmoving and providing no more fight. They all turned their attention to me, ignoring my fervent chanting.

"Now, let's break this one in. I got first." David unbuckled his pants and threw me to the ground. The others pried my legs apart so he could rip my pants from my body. He positioned himself to enter me and thrust his pelvis forward. I never felt his assault.

The blood ran from his face and he screamed in agony. David rolled off me and grasped at his penis, hands coming away bloodied. Large chards of wood stuck out from his member, one severing it to where it only held by a shred of skin and tissue.

My legs stretched, covering in hard, scaly bark. I felt protrusions jut from my hands and arms, stabbing at my captors and piercing them until they released me.

I stood on my newly transformed limbs and reached out with the sharp appendages, slicing the throat of one of the men and shredding the torso of another. I raised my heavily barked leg and brought the sharp end down on David's head, ramming it into him until all that was left was bloody pulp.

None of the men escaped untouched. Four were left barely alive at the end of my onslaught and through eyes grown heavy with bark and wood, I watched the clearing reject their offering of tainted blood and irredeemable souls. The ones who could still walk or crawl took their fallen brethren back into the woods as the spirits and life essence of the dead swirled around them on their way to hell.

Those men would not last the night before they joined them.

It was difficult for me to move as I continued to grow and my body became heavier and heavier. I forced myself to get to where Deecy lay in our purified clearing. I would not perform any of the lifegiving rituals I had learned. She would not have wanted that. Death was the only way she would ever experience freedom in her lifetime. It was the only way I would, as well. We had to die in this world and reawaken to another.

Her soul danced inside me and I picked up her corpse and held her. Continuously sprouting branches broke through her skin, tethering her corporeal existence to mine. Once she was entwined fully into my trunk, my feet rooted, right in the middle of our space.

Deecy continues to feed my body and soul with hers. My growth is nourished by her flesh and bones; my eternal spirit by the final achievement of our long sought, elusive freedom. I would share eternity with my beloved.

I recite poetry to her through my full branches, leaves murmuring with every breeze, accompanied by the singing of the birds: I will only love you better after death.

Paid in Full

"I need to get something for those fire ants out there." The heat of the coffee mug I held reminded me of those pests as I gazed out at my rose garden that morning. Turning my attention back to the newspaper, I saw her obscure ad, the tiny, nearly invisible print in the bottom corner of the raunchy propositions where only the desperately hungry would notice it:

I can give you what you want.

Payment expected in full at time of service.

I put on a scarf and sunglasses and drove to the address. She answered the door of the ramshackle tenement building with gnarled, rusted hands. She never spoke a word as she let me in through the tiny crack in the door.

I removed the scarf and rushed my words. "I want to be beautiful again. Please give me my hair back." The onset of menopause had cheated me of my birthright, my thick brown hair.

Her thick braids shone in the candlelight, seemingly too heavy for her bird's neck. There were no windows in the room, and no air circulating. The flames stood perfectly still, as she grinned a toothless grin and commenced to dig around in the old apron she wore around her sparse middle. I wasn't even sure she'd heard me, as she still hadn't acknowledged my request. I prepared to start over again in my most demanding mistress of the manor tone.

She blew out a candle closest to the mildewed wall and turned to me with her hand out. The dry whisper crawled past her cracked throat and seemed to hurt as it fell from her parched lips. "Now you will pay Mama Ziti."

I stared at her. Was she commanding *me* to do something, Shelia Fouchet, last in the long line of prestigious genteel blood, mixed as it was? I drew myself up to my haughtiest. *How dare the old heifer.*

"I will pay you when I get what I want." I spun on my heel and regally exited the apartment, allowing the door to slam shut behind me.

She'd learn.

The next morning found me gaping in the bathroom mirror. My rapidly spreading bald spot was gone. In its place was a mass of luxurious, thick, honey brown hair. I lifted each tress in my hands, examining each closely. It was real, and all mine. Each strand was securely anchored to my scalp. The crown was even more splendid than my hair had been previously.

I tossed my head from side to side, dazzled at how the light caught my hair and spun it from honey to gold. "Just wait till the girls see this!"

My wish was granted when the ladies at The Society ogled me rudely when I arrived for our monthly meeting. Their investigative perusals quickly turned to glares of envy when the verdict was handed down that the flowing locks atop my head were indeed natural rather than a tacky hairpiece or implants.

I was loving it.

My husband Burt, upon returning from New York, immediately ran his hands over my scalp and proceeded to make the most passionate love to me I've had in over ten years, murmuring over and over again, "Your hair is so beautiful. You're even more gorgeous than you were twenty-five years ago." He tugged my hair in passion, and exhilaration blew through me at the realization that he didn't end up with a handful of hair. He left for his latest business trip with promises on his lips to use my hair in ways I'd never thought imaginable.

I could hardly wait for his return.

I was sitting in front of the mirror preparing to brush my glorious hair, contemplating a revival of my career as a television journalist, or possibly even a young boyfriend, when I heard the dry whisper behind me.

"Now you will pay Mama Ziti."

I whirled from the vanity and found the skeletal old woman hovering in a corner of my bedroom with her hand out. *How did she find where I live?* My eyes darted frantically around the room as my mind ran rampant. I couldn't take a chance on her letting my secret out. Shelia Fouchet refused to be the laughingstock of The Society and I would not lose my husband now that I'd finally won him back.

I picked up the crystal make-up mirror from the vanity and rushed at her. I bashed her skull in, over and over, and I took a moment to note how little she bled, considering her head looked like ground sirloin. I jumped into my gardening clothes, tied my hair atop my head, and ran to the garage for one of the burlap sacks in which the fertilizer was delivered. She barely weighed sixty pounds, less than the fertilizer, and I was able to get her down the stairs and into my rose garden very easily. The thumping of her head on each step comforted me, beating like the tune of a Caribbean lullaby. I hummed along "Thump. Thump. Thump-thump-thump."

The gardeners took care of the estates' grounds, but the rose garden beneath my bedroom window was my own personal domain. I knew each bush intimately and relished the feel of the dirt beneath my hands when I worked there. I also knew which shrub would benefit most from the meager nourishment the witch would provide. I quickly dug a hole beneath the smallest of the bushes and threw her in. Even the thrill of gardening couldn't hold me—before long I was back in my bedroom brushing my mane.

I went back to my new favorite past-time, regaling myself with fantasies while I played in my hair.

The next morning, as I sat at the vanity to resume my ritual, I noticed that my mane was even thicker. And it looked more gorgeous. A glance in the hall mirror around noon showed that it had gotten fuller throughout the course of the morning. That night's grooming session revealed a small, hard protrusion sprouting from the spot where my hair grew in the thickest. Feeling a headache coming on, I immediately retired for the night.

I rolled from bed on the following sunrise and stumbled blindly toward the vanity. Through blurred eyes, I saw several of the lumps in the place of my honey colored tresses. I lifted my hands to my head choked on the scream that caught in my throat as I felt the thorns all over my head. My hands back, covered in blood. Shock sent me reeling backwards, but my feet wouldn't move me from in front of the mirror. They were rooted to the floor.

I stand here now, entertained only by the squirming of ant larvae feeding from the crevices between my extended flesh.

Now you will pay Mama Ziti.

The blood dried up long ago, leaving exposed meat for the ants to parade over, through, and under. Their incessant crunching and gnawing echoed through my head.

Now you will pay Mama.

I used to watch them, day in and day out, but not anymore. My vision has been reduced to milky, faint visions of a large rose bud growing from my right eye socket.

Now you will pay.

All Who are Sleeping Will Not be Awakened

Shango shouldn't have broken into the neighbor's yard again, no matter what he and Oshun saw that required extermination—no matter how good his reasons for doing so were.

"...may I see your dogs, please?" The animal control officer ended his official spiel with the question I almost didn't hear.

"Yes." I opened the front door wider so he could see behind where I stood. He jumped when he saw my two pit bulls sitting quietly just inside the house. Realization dawned as he understood they'd been there the whole time.

He quickly mopped his head, dripping sweat even at the late evening hour from the relentless Houston heat.

"Well...uh...they don't seem violent. If they were, they could've attacked me before now."

I nodded.

He pulled out a business card and extended it to me, watching Shango and Oshun the whole time.

"I have to make a report to follow up on your neighbor's call but everything looks to be in order. I see their shots are updated and you have them registered, so…"

Shango held his gaze and slowly closed the gap between him and the officer. Shango licked the officer's leg in the way I'd seen him do several times when someone wouldn't run from him in fear. When that someone was in pain. Shango then returned to the house and the officer's face twisted in confusion.

He laughed uneasily. "Big, friendly guy, isn't he?" He took a few steps closer to where we stood and both Shango and Oshun allowed him to pet them.

"I don't see any problem here." He pointed at the house next door, where I could see Elizabeth and Rand standing in their yard. "Just try to keep these friendly guys out of their yard, yeah? Some people are a little high strung."

He walked away and back towards where my neighbors stood. Elizabeth's screeches reached us before I closed the door.

"They bark so much! We can't even enjoy our yard because of them. I'm afraid for my children and myself. You need to take them away from there."

"High strung, indeed. That what they calling it these days?" I sucked my teeth and my animals huffed their agreement. We didn't need to stick around to hear the officer's response to her. We went back into our home to continue living our secluded life.

Oshun, Shango, and I were the neighbors usually forgotten about. No salespeople came to our door. We didn't attend the community parties and events. Children would trick or treat at our house on Halloween but we were invisible to their parents. I did most of our shopping online and I worked from home as an online educator. We didn't bother anyone and I only walked the dogs at night. Still, Elizabeth Barton hated us.

We'd been fixtures in the subdivision from the early days before the remaining lots were sold to a large builder. Our quiet little cul-de-sac then became home to three more families. The Bartons moved in and Rand came over to introduce himself. He was nice enough and their small children were cute. But we'd never be friends. His wife wouldn't hear of that.

The first time Shango got into their yard, Rand was at work. Low steady growls poured from Shango as he concentrated on the far corner of the broken fence. Shadows danced under the overcast sky. Sudden unease crept up my spine and I followed my dog into the yard, fixing my gaze at the corner where Shango stood.

Elizabeth came running out her back door with a broom and swatted at him. Still, he kept his back to her and growled, paying her no mind. I dragged him by his collar back towards our house, Elizabeth yelling the whole time behind us.

I agreed that he shouldn't have gotten in their yard. I apologized. I told her to send the fence repair people over with their invoice and I'd pay it directly. Still, she yelled. She insulted. And she threatened to call animal control. The babies followed her outside, crying at the commotion she was creating. She glared at us and took the kids inside.

The second time, she followed through and called the city on us. Frustrating as the visit had been, I knew there was no coincidence that the officer who came out needed healing. The energy surrounding him had been heavy, murky. The degrading of his energy was what drew Shango and Oshun to him, offering comfort and healing. When he walked away from us, his aura was already clearing, the darkness dissipating, hints of green replacing the black.

We had been back inside for about an hour when our doorbell rang. Rand stood on our porch, sheepish, holding a covered dish.

"Uh, Zion, I'm, uh, sorry about that whole scene from earlier. The kids and I made these for you." He held the dish out towards me. I smelled chocolate and sugar and guessed they were cookies.

I didn't reach to take it. Instead, I held his gaze until he lowered his eyes. "Did Elizabeth make these and send you over with them like a peace offering?"

He perked up, apparently thinking it was good I had determined the truth. "Yes. She did. And she told me to tell you she's also really sorry." The hand he held the plate in lowered slightly as I still didn't reach for them.

"No thank you. Rand, you know we'll never have any peace until she can get rid of us. And I won't let that happen." I did feel a twinge when I noticed the gray seeping into his usually yellow aura. "I really can't eat all those sweets. Tell the kids Shango, Oshun, and I really love that they made these for us and they can eat them for us as a return gift."

"She really isn't a bad person, Zion. She just gets highly passionate about some things." Rand didn't hold the cookies out again.

"You and the kids aren't bad people, Rand. Elizabeth is terrible. I hope her negative energy doesn't impact you and those babies too badly. I closed the door, leaving him standing on the porch.

Elizabeth Barton was a bonafide racist. She hated that her neighbors knew a Black woman lived next door to her, clearly able to afford the same luxury she imagined herself to live in. Her colors alternated between red and brown and nothing more. Elizabeth was always either completely self-absorbed or angry that everyone around her wasn't also as focused on her as she was herself. I didn't understand what Rand saw in her, but I already saw their small children developing their own, more positive personalities, and ignoring their mother's outbursts about the smallest things.

Cleaning staff rotated through their house on a regular basis as she insulted one group after another. One lady stopped coming after Elizabeth yelled at her for washing her hands in one of their indoor sinks. She insisted all help only use the hose outside for washing their hands. Another team stormed away from her porch without ever going inside to start working because Elizabeth exclaimed, loudly enough for the entire cul de sac to hear, "Do Black people even know how to clean well?"

She complained to the administrator of our neighborhood chat group that another neighbor had posted information about a Black Lives Matter healing event that was taking place in one of the recreation centers in the subdivision. She called the post inflammatory and divisive and demanded it be taken down, despite the well-publicized support the mayor and the police department gave the event.

She hated that our little circle was diverse and included families of different ethnicities. I often heard her shouting at Rand that he needed to hurry up and get her out of "the ghetto with these people", even though all of our homes were valued at several thousands of dollars above theirs. They needed to hurry and move. She was bringing much worse to our little neighborhood than decreased property values—she brought negative energy that grew more powerful each day she stayed and spewed her vitriol. I could only hope their home was the only one affected when it all spilled over.

I anxiously awaited their departure, however, I couldn't spend my time thinking about that hateful woman. I did worry about what she might do to Shango and Oshun. Oshun kept a polite distance, eyeing the house and yard warily but not going too close. But Shango was drawn to the darkness he intuited existed on and within that property. He never bothered the people, not even Elizabeth, only went into their yard repeatedly to threaten something unseen by the human occupants—something deadly.

"You have to leave that woman alone, boy." Shango stared at me in his way. He wouldn't stop going over there until he could flush out the darkness. It was a part of his job and he wouldn't rest until he had completed it.

The smell of smoke woke us up late that night. We checked our home, not finding the source. One glance at the house next door revealed what was burning. Shango and Oshun ran ahead of me as we all raced out into the street. Dark, heavy spirals of energy rose from their house and backyard, howling faces moaning over the crackling of burning wood and plastic. Disengaged arms reached into the house, swiping at whatever they could find to destroy.

Elizabeth's hate had finally spilled over and the dark energy wanted to consume everything it could.

Shango ran into the back yard, teeth bared, taking on the spirits he'd been tracking for weeks. Oshun and I ran into the house through the back door. Horned entities charged us, dissipating only when Oshun attacked them. They multiplied as we yelled through the house looking for the Bartons. We found the family upstairs, weakened by the onslaught of demons that worked to possess them. The children were left untouched, their innocence working as deterrents. Even though the spirits couldn't enter them, they did torment them, dancing around their heads and throwing things through the flames they stoked.

Rand lay almost passed out in the upstairs master bedroom. I shook him until he became alert enough to walk with a little assistance. I carried the children and prodded Rand down the stairs and out of the house. Oshun went into the other rooms when we got downstairs, weaving in and out of doors while nipping at entities on her way. Rand and the children and I stood out on the street, watching the flames shooting out of the roof of their home. I held the babies and kept him from going back into the house.

He was too weak to fight me and collapsed into tears against my shoulder, babbling. "What happened? Where's my wife? Are your dogs in there? Elizabeth!"

The baby girl pointed and whined at the spirits that began swirling over the house, submerging the structure in more darkness than the fire should have allowed. I understood that Shango and Oshun had a responsibility to exorcise the demons—but I worried about my loved ones.

Finally, both Oshun and Shango emerged, dragging an unconscious Elizabeth out into the street next to us. Rand fell down beside her and weakly tried to revive her. Firefighters arrived and started to put out the fire, perplexed at how fast the house was going up in the small amount of flames that were present.

Paramedics ushered the Barton family into their ambulances and drove away from the burning house. Their job was done once they got them to the hospital.

Shango and Oshun's jobs were concluded, as well. All that remained over and inside the house was true smoke. Every evil spirit had been evicted. As long as Elizabeth didn't move back in with her hate, they'd stay gone. Shango lost interest in the house and ambled back to our own abode.

We could only hope the next occupants wouldn't also usher in life-threatening negativity.

After a couple of days had passed, Rand rang our doorbell again. He looked haggard; his spirit heavy, gray now having overtaken his yellow color.

His mouth worked without any sound coming out. Oshun and Shango walked outside and licked him. He reached down to pet the both of them.

"I don't know what happened, Zion, or how to explain what I saw and felt the other night," he said when he found his words. "I do know I owe my family's lives to you and Shango and Oshun." He lowered his eyes. "Elizabeth said to thank you, as well."

"No, she didn't say that, Rand."

He sighed, the briefest hint of yellow starting to show on the outline of his coloring. "You're right. She didn't say that at all." He sighed, wearing the weight of the events on his soul.

I reached out and grabbed his hand, only willing to touch him and lend him my own healing energy when I saw that he was truly trying to reconcile with himself about his marriage.

"Elizabeth is lost to the darkness, Rand. She won't ever come to the light and wake up. As long as you and the babies stay with her, you'll be attacked constantly by the spirits of the night until you succumb to them. Even when her life was in danger and she was rescued, she couldn't let go of her hate."

Heavy tears fell down his face as his coloring continued to change to hints of green. "She's been telling people that your dogs caused the fire in our home. That you cursed her because you're a witch. I know that's not true. You all saved us. Even her. But she still has no gratitude. I took the kids and left her at her mother's house."

I gripped his hands in reassurance. "You and the babies will be okay, Rand. You're a good man. Once you sever your ties with Elizabeth, you'll be safe."

He nodded and wiped at his eyes, then reached down and pet the dogs one last time.

"If you or the dogs ever need anything, Zion, really, let me know. You can call me on my cell."

"You've already given us what we need. The energy is clear around here now. Let the sleeping stay asleep. Take care of yourself and those babies."

"I will."

Shango, Oshun, and I watched him walk slowly down the walk and towards the remains of his house. His three colors would stay intermingled for a while as he got himself together, but eventually, the gray and green would be replaced with his original yellow.

And Shango would stay in our yard while Rand tended to the clean-up and repairs. Until the next time he and Oshun saw something that needed extermination.

To Give Her Whatsoever She May Ask

Lord, please bless Your humble servant.

I grew up with prayers, praying every morning with my transplanted American mother and Trinidadian father. We kneeled at night before bed and gave the Lord thanks for each day that we finished. After my parents died, I prayed for their eternal souls. I'd even prayed for the kind of marriage I wanted and thought I needed.

My prayers had never been for a husband, specifically, though I knew one to be necessary to bring a child into the world the right way. I'd been a good Christian wife, respecting my husband and following his lead as head of the household. When he wanted me to quit working and tend home, I did it. When he was promoted at his job, I supported him.

I knew God wanted His children to be happily married, but it was likely not His plan for us to be unevenly yoked in misery. When Jorge told me he didn't love me anymore, he'd already stopped going to church and left the room anytime I put gospel music on the stereo. He asked me one last time to pray with him, and I prayed with him. He asked for guidance in the matter of our union and I silently prayed for a baby before he left me.

My most fervent prayer for a baby grew even more desperate as I crossed the threshold into forty years. All I'd ever wanted was children to nurse and cuddle and raise in the way the Lord desired of His children. I would only borrow them, because a true Christian knew they truly belonged to God.

By my forty second birthday, it looked like my most passionate pleas would be ignored. I didn't kneel so often by then. I was already the towns' crazy old woman. I kept mostly to myself and only went to market and town when absolutely necessary. And I travelled to Mr. Frank's cottage, down the hill, to work. Mrs. Frank had passed on five years ago, and now he was just waiting to join his wife in heaven.

I didn't have the heart to tell him that I suspected that there was no heaven, no God to answer prayers. I was tired of praying.

It was time to try something else.

I trudged down the hill to work, using the heavy stick I walked with to scout for snakes in the grass before they had a chance to strike. The sun had settled beneath the horizon, and the island was dark. I wasn't afraid, although the island folks didn't need much prompting to discuss their jumbies and other evil night spirits. I knew not to stop for strangers, and not to approach strange animals. I had my trusty pocket flashlight to spot predators.

What I had not been prepared for was the large ball of fire that slowly flew over my head. I expected heat, but instead felt an icy chill in its wake. I turned to watch where it would go next, transfixed by the way my womb ached as it passed, and my heart called after it. The ball circled my torso several times. I heard the coos of a baby and longed to touch the softness of its skin. I reached out and was overwhelmed with dread. I drew my hand back and turned on my flashlight. The ball rose upwards and dissipated.

I reached Mr. Franks' house to find him seated on the porch. He seldom came out, so I knew he must have been having a pretty good day.

"Good night, Ingrid."

"Good night, Mr. Franks."

He sucked his teeth. "Look, de spirits flying tonight."

"What are you talking about, Mr. Franks?"

"I glad you ain't run into one because it would probably take you away."

I thought about the ball of fire but didn't tell my employer.

"Dey looking for somebody to trick into taking dem on." His eyes gleamed with an unusual fervor.

"Come now, Mr. Frank. Let's get your dinner." I helped him up out of the chair and guided him into the house.

I usually took my dinner with him, but I had no appetite. I sat by the open window while he slowly ate.

A soft whimpering floated through the window. I looked at Mr. Franks, but he seemed not to notice it. It came again, louder, with cooing. I stood from the chair and headed to the door.

"No, Ingrid. Dat's no baby. Stay here."

"You hear that baby, too?"

"I hear what pretending to be a baby. Sit down, girl. Don't go by de door."

My feet obeyed him, but my heart thudded in my chest, making it hard to breathe I twisted my sweaty hands in my lap. *I can't leave that baby out there.*

"Girl, ain't nobody gonna leave no baby on de doorstep." Mr. Franks eyed me steadily. "I ready for bed, eh? I tired." With a strength I had not seen from him in years, he pushed his chair back from the table and walked to the door, where he flicked on the porch light.

On the way to the bedroom, he instructed me to pull some candles from the cupboard and light them.

I got him dressed and settled into bed and took my regular seat in the chair next to him. The flames flickered from the hallway and across the room.

"Why didn't you let me go to the door?" My arms still ached to hold the baby I'd heard.

"Dat was no baby. Dat was a soucouyant, trying to get you to open de door so she can come inside. She would have sucked you dry after you invite her in."

"You believe in those jumbies and things?"

"Yeah, girl, dey real." He spoke with conviction and fell off into a coughing fit.

"But don't they grant wishes, too?" I remembered all the stories my parents and town elders had told me my entire childhood. I believed them, too. The evil spirits could be used, if you were smart. Of course, a devout person would never entertain making acquaintance with the spirits and would instead pray them away.

"You gotta go look for dem and see where by de river dey leave dey skin, and if you take it, dey gonna beg to get dey skin back so dey grant you a wish." He reached out and grabbed my hand, and the years old calluses pressed against my skin.

"But dey is very dangerous. Don't mess wit dem, girl, please, because you more likely lose your life instead of get any wish. And even if you get a wish, it gonna be a payback." He squeezed my hand until it hurt. "You hear me girl? Topic done."

I sat in silence while Mr. Franks dozed off. He slept fitfully that night, opening his eyes and sitting up and glancing around the room until he saw me still in the chair. Then he would look at the candles, suck his teeth, and doze off again. I didn't want to alarm him by disappearing, so I didn't even leave the chair to do my regular nightly chores. Instead, I planned.

The next night, I left early for work and spotted the ball of fire rising above the trees alongside the river road. It floated towards me and began its slow circle. I didn't want the longing it created, because it left me feeling confused and hurt. I needed it to leave. I only wanted to get to the river side. I turned on my flashlight and pointed it directly at the ball until it repeated its disappearing act. I didn't know how long it would stay away and I had to complete my search before it came back.

I headed towards the area where I had seen the ball first rise and picked my way through the trees. The river side had sudden drop-offs into the water, and I didn't want to risk falling. Once I was deep enough into the brush, I turned my flashlight back on.

I searched the crevices of several rocks in that area. At the third group of stones, I stuck my hand inside the largest crack and my fingers brushed something that did not have the smooth feel of a rock. I lay the flashlight down and reached in with both hands. I pulled out an ornate jar, and even my untrained eye knew it was older than I could imagine. Energy thrummed through my hands where I held it. I pulled off the top and reached inside.

The object was soft to the touch, like silk, but much sturdier. It shone like gossamer in the faint light of the flashlight lying on the ground. I stretched it until the jar was empty. In miniature form, it looked like a tiny human body suit. I crammed it back into the jar and replaced the lid. Then, I tied the jar up inside my skirt, running to Mr. Franks' house.

"Girl, you lookin' sick. You need to go to your bed?" Mr. Franks eyed me.

I bent my head down and answered, "Yeah, I'm feeling sick."

He stared, eyes burning holes into me. "Go on to your bed. I can do fine tonight."

Before he could add anything, I walked away, remembering to pause and stumble occasionally as if I were really sick.

I was too excited to sleep. Instead, I sat on my porch, in the passing night, rubbing the jar like it was my personal wishing lamp. I thought daylight would never come.

Just as the birds were announcing the approach of dawn, the ball of fire appeared before me. I watched in awe as it shifted and grew into a beautiful woman.

"You have something of mine. Give it back." Her voice was low, almost a whisper.

Her beauty did not move me. "How badly do you want it?"

She saw I was going to stand my ground, and showed her true self. Wrinkles as deep as a penny settled on her face. Gnarled hands clenched at the ends of veiny arms bent up beside her shriveled breasts.

"So, you desire something of me before I can have my skin back?"

"I want a baby."

Her eyes widened, though I felt she was feigning surprise. "A baby?"

"That is my wish."

She glanced to her side, towards the river, where the sun was barely approaching the horizon.

"Fine. I grant you what you wish. Please give me my skin before I perish in the sunlight."

I held the jar closer to me. "How do I know you won't go back on your word?"

For a moment, her eyes held surprise, then her words came out in a rush. "I am bound to honor our agreement."

"I don't know…" I squinted and focused over her shoulder. I would know the walk of the figure behind her in my sleep. My ex-husband, Jorge, was coming up the hill towards the house. My heart told me I would have my wish, so I threw the jar towards the old woman and stood.

I didn't take notice of where she went after Jorge stepped onto the porch. In silence, he kissed me deeply and picked me up. We went to the bedroom that we'd shared as husband and wife. I couldn't call it lovemaking, since he never said a word and performed the steps as routinely as the sun rises. As soon as we were done, I knew I was pregnant. As quietly as he'd come, Jorge left. I never heard from him again.

Mr. Franks eyed me as my belly grew larger and I glowed with giddiness.

He screwed up his face and pointed at the baby jumper I was crocheting. "Why you want to get yourself in dis pickle with de child?" He sucked his teeth. "Dey don't do nothin but leech off you."

I focused my concentration on the jumper.

"Especially with Jorge gone. I heard he fell overboard out in the bay a year or so back and dey never found his body."

I focused harder.

"How long past since he come to de house, you say?"

Heat burned in my face. "Mr. Franks, my ex-husband paid me a visit and we got together. Now I'm with child. People do it all the time."

He sucked his teeth again. "Catch yourself, girl. Don't swell up your face so. I just hope you know what you're up against. Dat baby will suck you dry."

"That's what they're supposed to do, and I'll give it my all, willingly."

He never said anything else about it to me and pretended as if I wasn't growing bigger every day, though I saw the way he warily studied my belly. At seven months pregnant, I went in to work feeling terrible. No matter how much rest I got, I was exhausted.

"Girl, you got luggage under your eyes."

"You tell me, Mr. Franks? I'm tired." I collapsed onto the floor. I was barely conscious of Mr. Franks moving as quickly as he probably could, heading to his rotary dial phone to call for help. A knock at the door came from a distance.

"Who dat is?" Mr. Franks asked, and I heard the door open. "I can't hear you—" Mr. Franks' voice cut off in a high-pitched scream.

I willed my body to move, to find out what was happening to him, but I couldn't do anything but listen as the moist, ripping swallowing sounds continued. Then, a familiar face stood above me in a haze.

"You have to eat to feed the babies. They're too strong for your body. But you have to carry them as long as you can." Dry fingers pressed inside my mouth, opening it, and liquid warmth poured down my throat. The baby leapt inside my belly, making frantic movements all over. I settled into satisfied, but restless bliss. *What babies?*

When I awakened, I didn't see Mr. Franks in the house. The door stood open and rain poured down. I grabbed my walking stick and headed towards my house. I could barely see through the bales of rain. I crept along the muddy path up the hill, when my stomach was grabbed and squeezed in an unyielding fist. I doubled over and swerved towards the line of trees along the river road. Barely able to catch my breath, I stopped walking and searched for a safe place to rest.

Warm wetness engulfed my legs, heating the cool water that washed up my ankles. I reached down, my hand was covered in sticky, metallic smelling burgundy. I screamed. My babies' life flowed from inside me, passing through my body in thick clumps that forced my opening wider and wider.

Please save my baby.

Visions of destruction filled my head. I saw starving children and mushroomed clouds over large cities. Still frames showing desiccated bodies strewn without care ran like a slide show through my head. *Sometimes, death is God's will.*

I lost my footing and slid, feet first, towards the river.

Please save my baby.

I passed a still form, and my nose stung with the burn of decomposing flesh. I reached out to grasp something to stop my fall and held bones with small bits of flesh clinging to them. I recognized the rags surrounding the body as a shirt I'd bought for Jorge right before he'd left our home. He'd been wearing it when he'd visited me that last time. My mind grappled with what I was seeing as I continued to fall down the hill. I stopped after hitting my head on a large stone and slid into the rising water.

I'll give anything.

I reached down between my legs and felt the baby's head at my opening. The vice gripped my belly again and I grunted. My mind said I wouldn't push anymore, but my body did it automatically. I didn't have time to think about how dirty the river water might be, or what might be there with us. I pushed three times and the baby slid from my body, into the water. I grabbed it and held it close to me and tried to catch my breath. *A girl.* The next contraction expelled another body and I caught it in a one-handed grasp. *She said 'babies'.*

I had two daughters. Joy made the pain of giving birth fade. I pushed once again to expel the placenta, and wrapped the girls up in my folded, wet skirt. New pictures danced in my head, of children violated to the point of death and bodies drug behind vehicles. My head pounded with snapshots of torn torsos and human shaped burning pyres and screaming mothers kneeling beside the bodies of their children. My knees buckled.

Please save my babies.

The pictures slowed down until I slid into unconsciousness with the prayer to Whomever was listening dripping off my lips.

There was pounding at the door and I struggled to answer. My familiar bedroom came into view, and my daughters lay side by side in the crib. I pulled my body up and winced at the pains that lanced me. The knocking grew more insistent. I made my way to the door and opened it.

"Oh my God, Ingrid." Denise, my next closest neighbor, threw herself inside. "It's an awful thing, Mr. Franks and dem finally finding your Jorge."

Mr. Franks. An unbidden memory lingered just outside my consciousness. *Jorge.*

"Crazy how a body just wash up on de riverside like dat, over a year dead, too." She focused on me for the first time since she'd arrived. What happened to you, girl?" Denise stopped moaning. She reached out towards my chest and drew her hand back sharply. "Close your dressing gown. Were you attacked, too, like Mr. Franks?" Her mention of his name brought fresh drama from Ingrid.

I looked down and saw the purple and blue bruises on my breasts and up my chest. I realized I hadn't had a hard time waking up just because of exhaustion, but I couldn't open my eyes any wider without pain. They burned.

"I just had my babies, Denise. I'm tired. Tell me about Mr. Franks later when I up and about from my bed." I pushed Denise outside the door, against her protests. I leaned against the door until I could see her through the side window, on her way back down the hill.

The babies cried in the bedroom and my breasts tingled in response. The tingle stabbed into pain, and I watched as pink milk oozed onto the front of my dressing gown. By the time I made it to the babies, the pink had turned red and flowed freely from my breasts.

I settled down against the headboard with a baby underneath each arm and fed them. I caught my reflection in the dresser mirror and could barely recognize the drawn woman with sunken eyes and bruises all over. My skin was pale. Weak, I dropped one baby, but she did not loosen her latch on my breast. From the side pillow, she hung on and suckled harder. I could see blood dribbling down the side of her mouth.

"My deepest desire was for a baby, too."

I lifted my head to the hag standing beside the bed.

"I couldn't become pregnant, but I had the means to make you so. Corpses still have seeds and make perfect puppets to bend at will." She gazed at the babies.

"Our daughters are lovely. I will bring them up in the right way." She leaned over me. "I, too, answer prayers. But I demand an ultimate sacrifice. Feed them so that they may have everlasting life."

My last vision was of our daughters looking up at me with bloodied lips, as I faded. Tiny fingers clawed at my flesh and tore my body. I saw Jorge. I saw Mrs. Franks. Separately, I saw Mr. Franks. But I didn't know where we would be going, since there was no heaven. No God to answer prayers.

Queen of Monsters

Seemed pretty unladylike, un-Christian like, and downright un-queenly to deliver the children unto the monster. The monster didn't even eat the children all the way. He chewed on them, preying, and spit them out to be stomped in the ground. Hurt and broken. Dirty. Lonely. Blamed. Fatherless when family wouldn't believe the truth about family.

Maybe the so-called queen had missed her "Daddy" as she called him. I'm sure she did. Her husband had loved and spoiled her so. Big, silent, and kind to her small, bossy, and mean. We all missed my grandfather. We loved him immensely, because he was so wonderful--we didn't know he, alone, kept the monster at bay. When our protector expired, the beast thrived, fully birthed by imbibing the embers of our protector's dying breath.

Perhaps the self-titled queen was embarrassed to have given birth to the monster. Why was he always alone? Why did he insist on us children holding court around him every night in a darkened back bedroom? Surely, she wasn't so self-absorbed that she didn't see what everyone else saw: a strange man with no adult friends, unable to function in the disciplined world of marriage, the military, or the church.

The church was where she truly reigned, queen of all things Godly. She was a formidable teacher, forcing the prescriptions of ladyhood on us. I never said I wanted to be a lady, but she admonished me that I must. I never said I wanted to be a Christian, either, but no alternative was given.

Was it Christian to keep the monster's secrets? I don't know. I do know I was never Christian enough to forgive him his transgressions against me. I held my scourges buried in my heart, alongside the despair of being exiled by the queen, for sins not my own but hers and her monster's.

It was unladylike, un-Christian like, and un-queenly for me to curse someone. I embraced the anti-lady, non-queen, excommunicated Christian that I was, she who withstood the monster's attack and forged a sense of being that would transcend the mere mortality of the monsters—because that's what my grandmother really was: another monster. I would be here long after they, leaving my legacy while erasing theirs.

I cursed them both. I damned them to experience the loss of selfhood and the mental and spiritual anguish of a decimated childhood they'd relegated me to. I turned all my mental energy towards bringing pain and destruction to them. I wanted them tortured and broken before their deaths.

Then I waited to see the extent of the horrors that would befall them after I uttered their damnation.

But the curses were taking too long for me. I didn't have the patience of a lady because I was unladylike. I also couldn't allow my hatred to dissipate because I wasn't a Christian. I was, however, growing into my own kind of queen, one who understood punishment must be meted out to the monsters by she who reigned above all else. I had to relinquish the safety of uttered words and passionate energy and embrace my birthright. A queen should behave as a queen and take charge. I needed to act.

I went to him first, knowing full well he was still in that back bedroom, alone. Trying to shrink myself to hide from him as a child had worked sometimes and I used that hard-earned skill of invisibility to slide into the back door and down the back hallway to his room. It had previously been the Queen and my grandfather's room and I thought I felt his kind energy pass me in that small space.

I suddenly remembered how he'd walked down that same path, every single night, taking coffee into their room for him and his Baby. We had seen and felt him performing that same, comforting task, even after his death. He always disappeared before he got to the room door and I knew it was because he couldn't bear to face the evil that resided there then. An evil he had helped biologically spawn and that his wife had weaned on wickedness.

It affected me more than I could have thought. Gasping, I leaned against the wall, pleading with him to allow me my goal, to not try and stop me. I had suffered for so long and that was the only thing that would help me begin to find some kind of peace. The draft returned and embraced me, giving me his blessing to forge ahead. I used the energy to ease the door open.

The monster lay on a couch in the bedroom, one of only two pieces of furniture he had ever wanted in there. A full bed wouldn't have left room for him to insist we sleep in there on the floor. A nightstand and dresser would have removed the space he used to manipulate and abuse me. The light from the television, perched on a tiny table, shone on where he reclined in sleep.

He had never slept at night when he was torturing me.

Brandishing the straight-razor I brought along, I swiped it swiftly across his neck. I stabbed him in both sides of his torso so his lungs would be too punctured for him to take a breath deep enough to scream before he bled out. He had always remarked how tight I was, as if a child could be anything but, so I grabbed the flaccid weapon he had invaded me with. I laughed softly when he reflexively removed his hands from his throat to try to protect himself, the way I never could protect my private parts from him.

He was older and feebler than I remembered, a small man who I had outgrown, physically and mentally. I took my razor to his penis, slicing it off in one motion. I took the gnarled flesh and forced it between his lips, squeezing my hand over his futile gestures to scream and reject the pulp. I climbed on top of his body and pressed my full weight on his punctured lungs, wrapping my arms around him so he could look directly into my face, splattered with his blood, crushing his ribs and the air sacs underneath so hard I felt him break.

I whispered that I hoped my embrace was tight enough for him as he bled out.

I found her on the sofa in the living room where she'd started sleeping after my grandfather had passed away. She had always been tiny with long hair that cascaded down her shoulders. Age hadn't taken her crown of beauty away, only lightened it with full gray. I grabbed a handful of her hair and drug her off the sofa and onto the floor. Startled, she began to scream and thrash about. I placed a well-practiced round house kick to her head, not needed my full strength to stun her.

The monster had taught me that kick in the daytime when he couldn't bother me in other ways. She had only shaken her head at him and said it wasn't a good thing for a lady to learn.

I agreed, but that's why I continued to practice it on my own until I got really, really good at the move.

I drug her into the bedroom where her dead spawn lay, relishing in the pain crossing her face when she saw him. I yanked her up towards the couch, throwing down the handful of hair I had freed, and slammed her face into his crotch over and over again. He had raped me in life so he should rape her in death.

She was too weak to fight me and as much as I hated the thought of rushing the process, I knew I had to hurry and finish her before the kind soul of my grandfather appeared and tried to rescue her. He hadn't prevented me from killing the monster, but Baby? I wasn't sure he would allow that.

I drug her head up to the corner of the couch where the monster's blood had pooled up in the cushions. Pressing her face deep into the puddle of liquid, I held her there, telling her all the things he had done to me. I tilted her head up once so she could see my face. Was that a glint of pride I saw in her eyes, even as she started to fade? I pondered her expression and pushed her into the blood one last time, holding her head in place until she gurgled her last breath.

I cleaned myself up in our childhood bathroom, the one they always made us use so we wouldn't mess up the one company used. She had always taught us that if we could look our reflections in the mirror in the eyes at the end of the day, then we had done good that day. If we couldn't, that unsettling feeling we felt was our conscience, telling us we needed to do better the next day.

I held my own gaze comfortably. I determined that she had, at long last, finally been proud of me. Of what she had turned me into. She had willingly given up her throne to her successor: as selfish and relentless as she had once been, I was the new Queen of the monsters. My reign would be long.

I Would Have Rescued Them All

I *'m your sister.*

Kamyra approached the crying woman slowly, arms out to her sides as if readying for an embrace. She would give one if it was welcome.

I'm here to help you.

When she stood directly in front of the tombstone the woman sat on, Kamyra saw the intricate patterns of her cornrows, coiled around in knots on top of her head. The waning sun shone through those coils but Kamyra paid more attention to the grooves in the headstone that she could see clearly through the woman's lower body.

Do you want to sleep forever with our ancestors?

Finally, the other woman looked up. Translucent tears streamed down her face, never landing on the ragged dress she wore. *"Please."*

Kamyra placed her hand where the woman's shoulder appeared. She hadn't braced herself for the jolt of heat that raced through her, straight to her core. She doubled over and struggled to contain the spirit within her body for the duration of the process. Too much sadness. She cried out, relief resting just outside her consciousness that other people never wanted to walk in the places she did when it was so close to dark. No one could hear her work. Nor her torment.

When the despair eased, she planted her feet apart and raised her arms to the sky. *"Please accept our sister into your fold."*

The woman Kamyra had absorbed scratched her way up through her legs, swam past her innards, and emerged from her palms, swirling around her fingertips. *"Go in peace, my sister."* The spirit glided upwards until she dissipated in a puff.

A single tear escaped Kamyra's eye. Even when they wanted to go, they sometimes put up a fight she didn't expect.

She had a long night of work ahead of her.

She walked through the smaller path she'd seen once before in the cemetery. It was largely overgrown with weeds and surely forgotten by loved ones and town officials, alike. Something called her into those trees, beating inside her veins like the drums of ancient Africa. Squeezing her heart as if it wanted to take on its rhythm.

No spirits met her when she came to a clearing. Crumbled headstones formed haphazard shapes around the tree bases. When the entity slammed into her shoulders from above, she fell to the ground.

"You ain't no sister of mine!" The voice roared outside her head. Something wasn't right. They only ever spoke inside her head, her answers to them the same.

Kamyra whispered the incantation for protection. A ragged arm emerged from her torso, a large hand wriggling to re-enter her.

The words tumbled from her lips, her brain scrambling to remember the stronger appeal to the ancestors she had never needed before then, the regular request not expelling the entity quickly enough to prevent her further pain.

She implored again and found the spell in the vestiges of her brain, fuzzy as it was with pain.

The spirit pounced from her chest, whole. Angry. He charged her, growling. She drew a sigil in her palm with her spit and extended it towards the furious ghost. He recoiled and began stalking around her in a wide circle.

"You ain't no sister of mine!" He repeated this accusation.

Kamyra struggled to catch her breath. *"I want to help you."*

"I don't want your damned help. I got too much left to do!" He didn't bother to speak to her in the way of spirits. He continued to communicate as if he were still corporeal. He charged her again, his resulting recoil stronger, as

Kamyra regained some of her strength and brandished her sigil more boldly.

Mamaw taught her about these haints, these ones that didn't want to be dead and gathered strength in death. Kamyra had never encountered one in her work and she hoped she could send him on, too.

Failing to do so might mean her death.

She stretched out her free arm. *"Do you want to sleep forever with our ancestors?"*

"I hope dem ancestors is burning in hell! Dey ain't do nothing to help alla us. Dey talk about rebellion. Escaping. Caused dem folks to kill so many of us. All dey had to do was do what de folks say do. Continue to serve dem. We ain't had to die." He stopped pacing, looking her in the eye for the first time. "I ain't dyin' now.

He charged her again, sliding underneath her outstretched arm and into her lower body. Kamyra buckled, legs outstretched, as the entity surged throughout her body. He avoided the hand with her protection.

The entity forced her soul from its own encasing. She was suddenly surrounded by other spirits emerging from the soil.

He raised her unprotected hand and beckoned to his ghostly brethren. "Come wit me, my true brothers and sisters. We can continue our lives of service. Of survival. Come!"

Kamyra fervently started the one ritual she knew would work at this point. She didn't have any other remedies. It was tainted with dark magic and she was bound to never use dark magic on her brothers or sisters.

But that dude was no brother of hers, with all his talk of servitude.

"Our beloveds, I come to you as humbly as I know how. Please lend me your grace and your darkness! I beseech you!" Kamyra's soul screamed throughout the clearing. The broken headstones wobbled and rolled towards the entity inhabiting Kamyra's body, surrounding the flesh so it could not escape. Her body convulsed and twitched, falling to the dirt without the entity in residence.

Souls crowded outside the circle, reaching for the soul standing inside. He wailed, unable to get back inside the body and unable to leave the circle of punishment. Kamyra's spirit re-entered her body and slid beyond the stones.

Fire leapt from the fingertips of the spirits just outside the circle. Kamyra saw that these were more solid, more ancient, than those on the outer layers. These were her beloved ancestors. They made a barrier so their ignorant kindred stayed away from the fire, unharmed.

The spirit inside the circle burned, screaming in agony. Kamyra felt no pity for him. Neither did the ancestors. They continued to burn the fire until the afflicted spirit was disintegrated into nothingness.

Kamyra didn't know where he went. She didn't care. Her concern was her brethren whom she helped to ascend. She had never witnessed souls going elsewhere. It wasn't her path to send them there on her own.

She slowly carried her aching body to the outskirts of the circle as the ancestors started to dissipate. Each one opened their arms to one of the other spirits and took them along as they ascended. Kamyra approached the last two spirits.

"Do you want to sleep forever with our ancestors?"

They came into her willingly. She sent them into the night.

Kamyra sighed heavily. Aching, she re-traced her steps out of the clearing. The sun had gone down completely but she didn't need any outside light. She would see them when she needed to. It was her job.

She had a long night of work ahead of her.

Keep on Trucking

e and Sweet Thang done seen some crazy shit. I don't mean the regular kind of craziness that a 250-pound, six-foot, three-inch, Black queer woman with locs can fall into while she's pushing a big rig across the country. I mean, some real fucked up stuff. Mangled bodies sprawled across the roadways, severed, chewed limbs resting far from the main torso. Accidents unfolding on the freeway in slow motion, easily avoidable yet not. Lovers fighting in moving vehicles, swerving from lane to lane. Babies standing in laps inside cars bearing bumper stickers indicating, "Drive carefully, baby on board." Even that kind of damnable irony failed to shock me.

But nothing prepared me for that night on TX 239.

I still don't understand why my GPS took me that way to get to Dilley from Victoria, but I went along with it. If I ever got tired of driving, which was a long shot, maybe I could go work for the folks who programmed those things.

Getting a different set of directions every time I went somewhere got to be frustrating, especially when there were no traffic conditions or construction work areas that made sense. On that trip, I didn't have to pick up my load until the next morning and I learned a long time ago to just enjoy my time in the seat and not worry about what the GPS folks were doing. Sweet rode good and as long as I had my satellite radio and an endless stash of sunflower seeds, we'd take it on in.

I usually didn't expect to see much traffic on those backwoods, two lane highways in Texas, especially not at 3:30 in the morning. Most I'd see is a deer or a lost dog or five. Sometimes possums. Two legged creatures usually kept off those death trap roads with unseen curves and huge trucks, like Sweet pushing hard on top of them. I wouldn't see many people until I made it to the plant to pick up the load or if the sunflower seeds worked their fibrous magic and I had to make a run to a truck stop. Those were few and far between and I liked it best that way. Still, sometimes loneliness was my girlfriend in ways I could never keep a human woman.

They never stayed long when I explained how much time I had to spend on the road so I could help pay the bills. They wanted the money but they also wanted the time I just wasn't sure I was cut out to fit in. Last girlfriend I had spent our breakup discussion alternating between tears, while she fussed about my never being around, and fits of anger over how the light bill had doubled and I needed to pay it. I slid the bills from my money clip and handed them to her. Her eyes grew wide at the sight of the remaining bills. My own anger over how quickly she'd reduced me to just a sugar mama who paid for everything bubbled up in my throat. It didn't help that I'd told her that was kinda crazy because I was rarely ever there and didn't use the electricity. She told me to lose her number and I deserved that. I wanted to reflect on why I got mad at being perceived in exactly the way I put myself out there. Maybe later.

Sweet was the only woman I could commit to right then. She never asked me for anything except more gas...and the occasional opening up on the highway. I was glad to oblige. We were kindred spirits, me and Sweet. I couldn't articulate the freedom I found in the seat and on the road. My family hadn't traveled much when I was a child and I spent my childhood lost in books while my sperm donor beat up on Mama. I'd fantasized about life as an adventurer, traveling the world in search of good food and nice people. By the time I'd graduated high school, I'd given up on the nice people part. I barely made it out of there, that special circle of hell reserved for queer kids. Mama had already died of an aneurysm when I was fourteen and the sperm donor had pickled his liver pretty good. There was no way I was staying to take care of him. I left on the first thing smoking. That thing was a CDL training school and a few years later, I'd been able to invest in Sugar.

Seeing the first "Cemetery" sign made me think of the old man. I didn't know if he was alive or dead and we didn't have any family to let me know. I realized I hadn't ever seen so many roads marked "Cemetery" as I did on that highway that night. On both sides of the road, signs lit up telling me there were legions of dead folks off the main roadway. I couldn't see any houses. No signs of animal life beyond the border trees. I wondered how they could need so many cities for the dead when there didn't seem to be any living moving around in the first place.

I eased Sweet around a curve and slowed just a teench. No headlights, but I saw an inky shadow coming down the highway on the other side. I'd blast them with my high beams so they could hit their lights when they got closer to cross me. Would've been a shame to not let them know, just in case they really had forgotten to turn them on. Sometimes, folks let me know they hadn't forgotten and they were up to some kind of fuckery with the lights out on purpose. Those folks got me to ride on Sweet's loud, deep horn, while I flicked them the bird.

The shadow came closer, faster than I thought it was moving. I'm a good judge of distance and speed, but something wasn't working out with that. My bowels tightened and I automatically reached for the glove box for my piece. Then I drew my hand away. *Don't start none, won't be none.* A speeder didn't mean danger, necessarily.

My coily hair disagreed as the 4C strands that I hadn't had the barber shave away at the nape of my neck stood on end.

The blur moved closer and I made out a shape behind the wheel. Even in the pitch-blackness, the driver's white face came into view. Mostly mouth, the head swiveled in my direction and the car followed. At my speed, I couldn't stop Sweet in time and we made contact. The small two-door sedan flipped and went over the front end of my swiveled cab, landing behind my trailer.

It took a moment to figure out I was totally okay. The impact was lighter than I'd expected. No teeth rattling. No jarred bone sockets. The way the car flew over Sweet's cab…she would need some attention.

The driver probably needed way more attention than even Sweet. The car landed at an angle yards behind me and I needed to go check and see what I could do for the driver. I could see the sedan in my side mirror, just outside the back corner of my jackknifed, empty trailer. My taillights reflected off a crumpled driver side door. It looked real bad.

Then I saw someone walking along the road. Walking really wasn't the right word, but there was some kinda movement. The whole situation didn't feel right.

I picked up my cell phone to dial for assistance and was greeted with "No signal". Panic rolled up inside me and I fumbled for my CB. No one answered there, either. The level of shit I was in when even the CB wouldn't work hadn't quite registered. I pushed the thought to the back of my head and figured I would have to check and see if the driver had a cell phone. I pressed Sweet's handle so I could go help that poor soul. I'd seen dead bodies many times before and it never got easier. I prepared myself for the gore and tried to take calming breaths.

The willowy white shape of a person that I'd been willing to relegate to my imagination before flickered in the side mirror. As I watched, it folded onto two wobbly legs, impossibly long. Arms stretched out in awkward positions, and the head remained tilted to the side as if it couldn't lift it. I looked around for a house or another vehicle. That dude couldn't have come from the sedan I'd hit because that driver wouldn't have survived the crash like that, much less have been able to move around outside the car.

The broken man Crip Walked to a funky beat I wasn't feeling, legs jumbled and crooked but still moving, supporting a body that looked barely held together by whatever he was wearing. He came closer. My mistake: he wasn't wearing anything, barely even a face. The mouth I'd seen before he careened into Sweet was gone, replaced by a swirling hole that looked almost like the drain on a sink, but growing bigger. His arms elongated and shrank, in opposition to his legs, which ballooned out at a steady pace. I saw no eyes, but I know he saw me.

Though he didn't appear to be wearing clothes, I couldn't see any other body parts beyond a head and appendages. He glowed. And even from inside the truck, I could feel the heat being sucked out all around the outside of the cab. A wet thud shook the truck and I jumped.

White fingers crept along the side windows, reaching and reaching. A stretched torso followed arms. Swirling hurricane holes covered Sweet's windows everywhere the thing touched. I heard small creaks and watched tiny webs begin across the glass.

I reached for my piece again. The tilted head appeared in my cab window, almost at the top of the 14-foot roof. White arms continued to ooze across the windshield and locked together at the other window. The glove box jammed; the metal latch too cold to manipulate. I probably had something I could fight with in the sleeper, but I couldn't move to get back there. The temperature continued to drop in the cab.

I never froze in the face of danger, but I was scared shitless right then and literally frozen in place. The glove box finally opened for me and I fumbled with my gun with frozen fingers while Sweet whimpered, creaking underneath the icy crush assaulting her.

Headlights shone through the white figure and it was suddenly gone. I caught my breath and could finally breathe air warm enough to not slice my lungs with frozen blades. A light-colored pickup truck had stopped a few yards away from my cab. I wanted to yell out the window to warn the driver. I looked around for the monster and didn't see it. I wasn't sure if maybe it had nested on top of the truck and was waiting for me to get out.

None of that mattered when the driver walked toward my truck. A white blur oozed over him, turning pink and gelatinous, pulsating over the man. I rolled the window down to fire a warning shot, knowing I couldn't just shoot the creature without also shooting the man it was devouring…absorbing? I don't know what the hell it was doing but I had to do something.

My doing something didn't matter, either, when the creature resumed its position wrapped around Sweet. The cold intensified more than before, creating frost on the inside of my windows. The light sprinkling couldn't hide the bits of sinew and flesh that moved along the glass within the monster. Teeth and bone scraped along, clinking along the window, pressing into the fine cracks that continued to spread.

Transfixed, I shivered uncontrollably. *How can it move and still be frozen like ice?* It looked like ice but had the slow movement of half-done gelatin. I could feel the blood slowing in my veins, the unbearable cold also slowing down my brain. It took a while to figure out the red and blue filtering through the windows could be from a police car. For the second time, the creature abandoned me and Sweet and disappeared. There was a police car in the mirror.

Breath stopping terror and freezing numbness couldn't quell the secondary fear that took root in my consciousness. Years of growing up Black in Texas caught up to me when I heard the officer tell me over the loudspeaker to get out of the truck. I still held my gun clasped in my thawing hand. I had to do what he said. Right away. In that moment, I wasn't sure if I'd rather be attacked by the monster or shot by the officer. Man, I was in a bad spot. I reluctantly opened the door to my truck.

Slowly, I complied with the officer's command, trying to keep my one hand on the rail as I climbed down, gun safety on, piece hanging from my finger on the other hand, raised in surrender. My life was still in a precarious position but I needed to warn the officer, too. We both had to get out of there.

I walked toward the officer, with my hands in the air. Dread crept in again as the temperature began to drop quickly. "Officer," I shouted, "There's danger…"

In an impossibly short time, he stood face to face with me. Despite the darkness, I saw his white face, plainly. He was a tall man and I had to look up at him, which was unusual. I'm a big and tall woman but he easily had a head on me. He spoke, without a Texan accent. "What happened?"

"Officer, I have a weapon…" Self-disclosure had always seemed the best thing to do when I was stopped by law enforcement, even though they could have run my plates and found that I'm a registered gun owner. Disclosing that didn't seem helpful then. The officer didn't even have a gun, himself, and he never even glanced at mine hanging above my head.

"What happened?" he repeated.

"There was an accident. That car ran into me, head first. The driver can't have made it okay. But…" I struggled for words. Even African American Vernacular English failed me at that point. I couldn't just tell the officer, "It's some fucked up ass shit popping off in this joint!"

"You saw the driver?" He squinted his already small eyes, turning them into the barest of slits in his face, perched above a flat nose and thin lips. All his features were way too small for his long, narrow head.

"I did. He was tall. And white." *Like you.* I tried to read his badge but it didn't glow the way his pale skin did.

We both turned at a flurry of movement off to my left side. A blur of white passed alongside the wrecked car. I shivered.

The officer swung my way again. "Take this card. Go to this body shop. They'll fix your truck up."

"Sir, there's a monster out here. You should get back up. I can help you."

"You can't help me. You need to get out of here." He spat into the darkness. "Go, on."

By the time he handed me the card, my teeth chattered and a jolt of icy fear stroked my spine. Where our fingers met, I felt the stab of mind shattering pain. I jerked back and pressed my injured hand against my body. I could barely move my frozen joints but fear and pain have a way of providing compelling motivation in times like that.

I spun around awkwardly, moving away from the officer, still not sure he wouldn't produce a gun and shoot me in the back. I couldn't have said if I was more afraid of him, the cold, or the dude he was looking for.

"Go!" the officer yelled from behind me. I broke out into a lumbering jog. From my side vision, the lawman lunged towards the white blur. My black ass went on. I climbed back up into my truck.

I was definitely most afraid of the dude he had found.

Sweet must have been as ready to go as I was because she cranked right up despite the frigid iciness that still gripped us. It took longer than I would have liked to get the cab and trailer back in line. It didn't help that I caught flashes of the officer and the other dude, blurs of white, in the side view mirror as I navigated. My hand burned with a steady, icy pain that jolted past my elbow and danced into my shoulder.

Once we got straight in the road, I burned off. I refused to even slow until I saw the first crossroad and turned off TX 239. Then, I pulled over to put the address from the card into my GPS. I also took a brief moment to examine my hand. I couldn't see anything on it, but it hurt so bad my vision blurred. I didn't think I'd ever get warm again.

I considered taking my gun into the dilapidated body shop with me. Sweet's clock said it was only 5:45am and the place was lit up like it was the middle of the day. Might not have been the best way to get the answers I needed, though, so I left the piece as I entered the humidity swollen wood door.

"Help you?" The tiny old woman behind the desk didn't look up. Her voice sounded like the rasp of dry dust, rubbed against newspaper.

Everything I thought to say stuck in my throat. It was too crazy to tell somebody else. I still had to get Sweet fixed up, though, so me and my insurance company would just have to take the "L" and eat the accident costs. I didn't have a police report number. I didn't even have the other driver's insurance info.

"An officer gave me your card."

The lady peered up at me over the top rim of her glasses. She flicked her eyes over the card, over the two, large red marks now covering my two of my fingertips and bleeding over brown fingers. I turned my hand over in front of my eyes. Those spots hadn't been there before, but right then they almost glowed, beaconing to the world where the pain invaded my body so harshly I thought I was losing the fight.

"Unh hunh. Watcha driving?"

"Rig outside. Accident. I hit…"

"I know." She eased her body from the chair behind the counter and pressed a button on the wall behind her.

I stood, silent, waiting for her to speak again. She didn't.

"I have insurance information to give you, too." I tried to reach for my back pocket but her pinned gaze stopped me.

"No need. Don't want it." She glanced at my hand where I held it pressed against my bosom while my knees threatened to buckle. "All we want is for you to get fixed on up and get outta here." She nodded. "They done marked you. Why they saved you, I don't know. You'll figure it out. But you gotta get on down the road."

I shivered harder, never having stopped since I drove away from the accident scene. The air around me wasn't cold, but I was freezing.

"You can try to put some ice on your hand. It'll ease the pain somewhat, but it'll always throb and ache. Won't never heal all the way up. Always be there." She slid a key attached to an old-fashioned key fob across the counter and I saw the same red markings along her arm, travelling up to the bottom of her sleeve. "No truck stop, but we have rooms out back where you can rest and wash up. Truck'll be ready in about six hours. Take your eight and then you'll leave."

I took the key with my good hand and nodded. She spat snuff infused spittle into a spit can on the corner of her desk.

I would gladly leave, take Sweet, and go. Forever marked. Keep on trucking.

The Lost

I went to see Eddie at the diner on the corner. The days had already gotten shorter and I wanted to get back home before it was completely dark. Dwayne. Just the thought of my husband warmed me momentarily, as I smiled at the remembrance of his face. Then the wind blew and I pulled my coat tighter around my body and went into the diner. My coat barely fit around my blossoming belly but I proudly wore my too small covering. The baby and I needed to go home to be with my biggest baby as soon as we could.

I felt Eddie over in the corner before I really saw him. He emanated an oily, slick odor and degenerative energy. As I approached him, he looked me up and down like he wanted to take a bite out of me. That look had always freaked me out, since my late teenaged years, when I'd stupidly slept with him. That had been a huge mistake, one I forgave myself for because he had preyed on me as soon as I turned of age. Obviously, having kept him as my manager had turned out to be the worst mistake.

"What's up, baby?" He put his cigarette down in the ashtray in front of him and made as if to stand. I shooed him back down into his chair and remained standing. He scratched at his already well marked face, drawing my attention to the fresh sores on what had once been dark, smooth skin. His gaze darted around the room as he tweaked.

"I'm not here for the small talk, Eddie. You know why I'm here." I still felt the chill of outside and shuddered as his cool dark eyes never left my face and he fidgeted more in his chair.

He went from zero to sixty, as he was prone to do when he was coming down off his high. "You still on this firing me kick?" He picked the cigarette back up and took a quick drag. I recognized the look in his eyes and I just wanted to leave before he got fully cranked up and agitated.

"Eddie, you know I have to. You completely screwed up the last show. My paintings weren't there on time, no one showed up, and you totally made sure that I can never show at Martha's again with that good little, undeserved cussing out you gave her. And besides that," I sipped at the warm inviting coffee he'd ordered for me before I arrived, "you're using again."

He started to say something and I cut him off. "You and I weren't good as lovers when I was too young to know any better, and I never held that against you. But you always were a good manager. A natural hustler when you aren't using. I got to cut you loose. There's too much at stake now for me to give you another chance. You're lost and I don't know if you care enough to ever be found." I drank more of my coffee and watched his face turn from ill-feigned cool indifference to mottled anger.

"You wouldn't be shit if it wasn't for all my hook-ups. You get a little piece of change and now you think you better than me? I made your bougie ass, Tee, and you might not want to forget it." He sniffed and wiped his chapped nose on his sleeve. "Now about the next show, I was thinking…"

I put the coffee mug down. "Don't bother. I mean what I said. This is over. Try to get clean and get back on the grind." I turned to leave the diner. I had felt bad at first about having to sever ties with Eddie because we had known each other for so long, but he had made his bed and he'd have to lie in it with his fleas.

I had to get home. The entrance to the alleyway loomed at my side. I could have gotten to my apartment five minutes faster if I would just jet through there really quick. I chuckled, knowing I couldn't do much of anything really quick with my six months preggo belly weighing me down and making me clumsy. But I made the last-minute decision to veer right, turning into the mouth of the short cut.

About halfway through, I stumbled on something beneath me. My left leg buckled and as soon as I hit the concrete, pain exploded in my head. It felt like a vice was tightening on my skull and I had to lay in the cold for long moments to keep the impending nausea at bay. I suffered from migraines, even during pregnancy, but that headache was different. I resolved to have Dwayne take me to the emergency room when I got home because I was worried about the baby after hitting my head that hard on the ground.

He would fuss at me for having left my cell phone at home to go fire Eddie and I hoped he would do so quietly. Even when the pain started to fade slightly, I still felt sluggish and any movement on my part resulted in waves of exhaustion. I tried to turn my head around to see if anyone was walking nearby whom I could signal for help. There was nothing in the alley except me and a large brick just at the periphery of my vision. Finally, I managed to stand up unsteadily and I stumbled forward, my vision blurring into nothingness and my instincts set on home.

I felt the sheets under my cheek as I shook my head slightly to try and clear my thoughts. I saw outside the window of my bedroom. It was already dark. I sensed Dwayne nearby, and the warmth that flooded me got my body moving. Padding silently out of the bed, I went to look for him. I found him in the bathtub, his head hanging back on the tub. Poor baby. He was always so tired. I slid into the bathwater on top of him and nestled his head to my breasts.

"Tessa, baby. I missed you," he murmured, and began to kiss my breasts. I felt him become aroused and immediately took him inside me. We rode together until we both were breathless and his skin turned goose pimply from the cold water. The pain in my head abated slightly while we loved on each other. Then we returned to the bed where I instantly fell asleep again. He made me feel so alive, so warm. We would have to take time to really talk the next day. I'd clear my schedule so I could be home with him in the morning.

The next day, I woke right at sunrise. Dwayne was already gone to work. I could still feel the headache throbbing at the base of my skull and struggled to get out of bed so I could get ready for the day, but my limbs felt like jelly. I realized it was useless to try anymore to get out of bed, and just went back to sleep to sleep off the headache. I dreamed of endless fields of bluebonnets, like the ones where Granny used to take my sister and me on picnics. The flowers were beautiful, much more so than I was ever able to make them in my paintings. A plump baby cooed and I picked her up to throw kisses on her tummy. She looked just like my sister had as a baby. I sat her down again and laughed as she scooted off through the field, grabbing at bluebonnets along her way.

When I awakened again, it was dusk. I heard Dwayne downstairs and I went to see what he was doing. He was sitting in his favorite chair with a drink hanging from his hand. The rush of desire that always came with the sight of my husband overtook me and instead of saying anything to him, I simply sat in his lap, straddling him. We could talk later. The headache had given me a reprieve and I would make the best of it. I could never get enough of that man.

His hands circled my waist as he pulled me up and down on him. I felt the crescendo rising and bubbling up inside me until I felt I was breaking into pieces. We tumbled into the couch and I heard Dwayne snoring. That night I dreamed of bluebonnet fields again and the little girl who looked just like my sister. She was a pretty toddler. She picked the flowers and handed them to me, one by one. Each flower was bolder and bluer than the next. Then she toddled further into the field until I couldn't see her anymore.

I forced my eyes open so I could get up. I couldn't remember how long I had had the headache and had lost track of time. That wasn't the first time that had happened, since I occasionally suffered from pregnancy brain, but it was the first time in a long while. I heard a droning sound in my ears, like voices. Dwayne's voice became clear. And a woman's voice. Who was that? I forced myself to get up from the couch. My body felt like gelatin and every movement was torture, but I had to see who was in my house. Dwayne wouldn't dare cheat—he loved me. I turned to see where the voices were coming from and I saw Dwayne sitting at the kitchen table, with his head in his hands.

"Dwayne, this isn't healthy. It's already been six months." I had never seen her before, but the way she stroked his bald head made the anger in me rise instantly.

She wanted him and he allowed her to continue her forward gestures.

Dwayne didn't move away from her touch and his voice held sorrow. "I can't let her go. She was my whole world. I still feel her here."

I slowly walked toward the table where they sat. The woman continued stroking his head, making comforting noises as he began to weep deeply from his soul. I caught a glimpse of a tattered newspaper on the bar. "Suspect in Murder of Up and Coming Artist Found Slain. My press picture was posted beneath the headlines. So was Eddie's.

Dwayne spoke again. "All I ever wanted was for her to have my babies and be with me forever. Now I've lost the baby and her."

The baby. I had left my baby in the bluebonnet field. I needed to go find her. Dwayne would call for me again soon, always, and I would always be there. At that moment, I had to find our baby girl. She needed her mommy in the daytime, to run and play in the bluebonnet fields with her.

Thinking of the fields transported me to them, to her. She knelt down at the side of a depression in the field, studying the depths intently. When she saw me, her face lit up.

"Mommy!" She ran over to where I stood, no longer a toddler, but an adolescent, starting to look more like me as she grew.

"I was scared you were lost." I hugged her tightly. She wiggled in my grasp.

"I'll never be lost, Mommy. I'll always be with you." She pointed to the spot where she had been kneeling. "But that ugly man? He'll always be lost."

Allowing her to drag me through the flowers, I looked down to see a man's form scrambling around a moderately deep hole in the ground. Bite and slash marks crossed his naked body. Open sores oozed alongside the marks and ants feasted on the secretions and flesh. His mouth opened but no sound came out. When he saw me standing at the top of the hole, he rushed to the side where we stood.

Eddie made a weak attempt to climb out of the hole, raising one of his sore riddled hands towards me. My daughter bent over the edge of the hole and grabbed his flailing hand, biting one of his fingers off. His face contorted in pain. She swiped at the hand that held onto the soil and bloody slashes appeared where she touched him. Seemingly chastened, he fell back into the hole and wept tearlessly.

"I'll always find him, though, Mommy. You go be with Daddy. He's calling you again. We can't let him think we're lost, too."

Bloodline

I woke up in a puddle of breast milk. I struggled against the bulk of my belly to sit up and shake away the nightmare. The baby did a series of flip-flops in response to my pounding heart. Despite the lingering terror of the dream, I smiled.

I placed my hand against my belly and was rewarded by a sharp kick, then another. Baby Tommy was always so active! I let out a long breath. I was having contractions, but I wouldn't bother with timing them just yet. The nightmare, which was the same as it had been since the beginning of my pregnancy, still held me in its throes.

I lay in a hospital bed, holding my new son after his delivery. I delighted in watching him squirm in my arms, as I checked him over and over for all his body parts. Then, Mama walked in the door. Daddy followed close behind her, dressed in the same overalls he'd worn ever since I'd been aware of it.

However, the look on his face was different. He didn't wear the calm and complacent features he usually did. He looked giddy and excited, almost bursting from his skin. I thought he was just excited about the birth of his grandson, but I immediately dismissed that thought. He hadn't been that excited about the birth of Colleen's baby, and she was his favorite child after all.

The nurse came into the room to check on the baby and me. As soon as she left the room, Daddy pounced on me and snatched the baby from my arms. Then he threw back his head and swallowed my baby boy whole, blanket, cap and all. "Daddy, Daddy! Don't eat my baby!" I would sob. Then I'd wake up at that point, with my heart threatening to pound out of my chest. Just like tonight.

I waddled to the kitchen for a glass of water since I was already awake. I tried to rub the pain from my back as I walked. The balmy swamp air engulfed me as I hit the open kitchen. The curtain at the window barely moved in response to the slight breeze coming through the trees toward our little cabin. Across the swamp I could see the lights still on at Mama and Daddy's place.

They kept late hours, finishing up the quilts and blankets we handcrafted and sold in town. Mosquitoes buzzed around the window, as if they knew I was there, and wanted my blood. It was all a show, though. We Teaks had swamp water running through our veins. The bugs wouldn't bite me any more than the alligators swimming around our cabin tried to eat us. We could practically swim alongside them and they'd never even turn our way.

At least that's what Maw Maw always said. She was well over one hundred years old, and knew everything, although I never wanted to test any of her theories. I just took her at her word. Just as I took her at her word that she and Mama would deliver Tommy Jr. with no problems right here at home.

I padded painfully back to the bedroom, still trying to get rid of the ache in my lower back and rolled into bed. Tommy hadn't moved an inch from his spot smack in the middle of the bed. I ran my hand over his sinewy arms, and around to his bare chest, over the little birthmark sitting there, that we both shared. I felt only a little warmth for him as my husband, but passion between us wasn't a necessity.

Tommy was my cousin, twice removed, and I'd grown up playing with him here in our swamp. Our parents arranged our union, just as their parents before them had arranged theirs, and Mama said I couldn't expect to be madly in love with him. She said I wasn't supposed to be, that marriage wasn't about love. It was about keeping the bloodline going, and the only way we could do that was by marrying back into our family. Sort of like the royal family.

I didn't bother to wake Tommy, because he'd just say the same thing he always said when I tried to tell him about the dream, which was the same thing Mama had said. "That's crazy, Jeannie." She never once looked up from the quilt she was working on, her brown, heavily veined hands flying with the needle.

"The idea of you having that baby in a hospital. You know Maw Maw and me are gonna get that boy out right here at home." Then she'd snorted. "Them doctors don't know anything anyway. Got all we need for birthin' and doctorin' right here in our swamp."

We rarely went outside the swamp for anything. Daddy and Tommy and a few other men went into town once every couple of months to sell the crafts we'd worked on and bought supplies while they were out. Tommy had always brought me the latest magazines and a few books when he came back, ever since we were children.

The magazines were already a few months old by the time they reached town, but they were my link to life outside the swamp. And having their little knowledge made me love the swamp even more. In his own way Tommy knew I was a little different from the rest of them, but he didn't hold it against me. Besides, I never expressed any interest in leaving the swamp.

The swamp spoke to me in its own language. The animals were unique to our waters, and the plants all stood up at attention when I passed by. The mossy curtains hanging from the trees over the water lent themselves to a romantic air, heightened by the humidity that always hung over us. We were completely separated from the rest of the world, and I loved it.

I would go out during a rainstorm just to watch the havoc the wind wreaked on the trees overhead, and how tranquil the swamp below remained because of the density of those trees. And when the bugs joined in, that was a real treat. Their chirping and clacking and buzzing made the most beautiful music in our little world. I was right at home in the isolation of my swamp.

But there was no music tonight. All was quiet in my swamp, except for the buzzing mosquitoes, their restlessness matching mine as I tried to get back to sleep and found that I couldn't. My back ached, and the baby was especially busy now that I'd awakened him. Just as I thought I could finally drift off; I felt a wetness between my legs. Then I was wracked by a painful contraction that doubled me over. I reached for Tommy to find that he was already pulling on his overalls.

"I think it's time," I grated from between clenched teeth.

"I know. I'll go get your folks." But just as he had been alerted, they had too. The three of them, Mama, Maw Maw, and Daddy came walking through the door of our cabin just as Tommy made it to the door of our room. They threw their supplies in the chair by the bed, and I chanced a look at Daddy as he began to lead Tommy out of the room. He looked just as calm as he'd always been. Chiding myself for being foolish, I got ready to weather another contraction while Maw Maw readied me for the delivery.

"Is this supposed to happen so fast?" I panted.

Mama patted my back. "Yes, child. You've got a body for birthin' babies. You'll have a short but hard delivery. Don't you want that boy out of there?"

I nodded and began the hard work of getting Tommy Jr. born. Within a couple of hours, Maw Maw was announcing his arrival, and held him up for me to see.

He didn't look as big as I would have expected, with the large size of my stomach. But I was still having contractions and couldn't concentrate on him just yet. Mama reached over for the baby and went to clean him up. Then Maw Maw was telling me to push more, and I was ready for the afterbirth to be out, too. But she grinned her toothless grin and held up a second baby.

"Isn't she a beauty?" she crooned, as she handed her to Mama. Twins! That's why it always felt like the baby was doing extra somersaults in there. I smiled weakly and pushed the remainder of the tissue out into the basin Maw Maw held beneath me.

"Mama, can I hold them now?" I was anxious to get my babies in my arms.

Mama ignored me and busied herself with the babies and then went out the door toward the front room.

"Hush now, child. You need to let me get you all done here." Maw Maw hurriedly decided I didn't need any stitches and began to clean me up. Mama came back into the room, followed by Tommy and Daddy. Daddy was his calm self, trying to calm a now excited Tommy. Mama brought the babies over to them and handed one to Tommy and one to Daddy.

"Here Tommy, meet your daughter. And Daddy, meet your bloodline." Daddy took my son by one foot and tore off his shirt and overalls with his free hand. A large gaping mouth with razor sharp teeth opened from the middle of his chest and he bent over backward so that it could open wider. He lifted my son over the opening, and began to slowly feed him in. There was no crying, no blood.

Afterward, Daddy danced around in restless excitement. "Thomasine, you never told me it was that good! I really missed out when you insisted on going first with Colleen's."

Too stunned to speak. I weakly tried to get out of the bed to get to my daughter, whom Tommy was holding tightly in his arms. She'd begun to squirm and Mama went over to where he stood.

"Be quiet, Herschel," Mama said. "You're exciting the boy. Tommy, I know it's hard right now, but you'll get your turn when little Tammy has her children. That's the way it is, the way it's always been. One's for keeping, and the other's for eating." She bent over the basin that held the placenta and tore off a bit. She unbuttoned Tommy's shirt around the baby, and then fed in the bit of tissue. He was instantly gratified. "That ought to last you, boy, until it's your turn to feed." Then they all whirled toward me. I'd begun to cry softly.

"Jeannie, don't be upset. This is our way." Mama had retained a bit of the tissue she'd fed Tommy Sr. and worked my gown up until my birthmark was exposed. She pressed the tissue to the spot and I watched as it opened, and small teeth protruded from around the mark. The teeth grated until the tissue was gone.

I felt soothed, then, and settled back into my pillows as Mama rearranged my gown. After all, I'd only expected one baby.

A Woman's Work

J amarcus was on that crazy tip before he hit the door. I could smell it on him, underneath the sweat that drenched his dingy wife beater tee.

He clumped into the kitchen, sucking his teeth. "Hamburger again?" He slammed a plastic grocery bag of empty, stinking food containers into the sink, ignoring the clean dishes already there.

Ten years of marriage had taught me that the conversation could go badly, whether I answered or not. I remained silent.

"You don't hear me?"

My neck prickled from the fire bubbling inside my skin. "The whole block hears you."

I turned from the sink and faced him. He needed to back off. He didn't always. Jamarcus was a handsome man, with chocolate colored skin that stretched over tight muscles and gleamed from his long day at work. I had loved him dearly once, warts and all. But I was getting tired of his shit.

He stared at me a moment and threw himself into a chair like a petulant child. "I work hard, you know. I'm sick of eating the same old thing every night."

"It's the best I can do, Jamarcus, when you spend money we don't have on that bike of yours." I placed a plate with the hamburger meat and macaroni in front of him.

"Oh, I'm *gonna* get my bike tricked out. And you nagging won't stop me from going to Bike Week next month, either."

"Do I ever nag you, Jamarcus? You do whatever you want all the time and I don't say a word." He wouldn't meet my eyes and mumbled under his breath instead.

I held myself in check long enough to gently set a glass of ice on the table next to him, along with a pitcher of fruit punch. A roach scurried underneath my feet as I walked down the hall towards the children's room.

The furious tears I'd held at bay slipped down my face as I ran my hand along our oldest son's cheek. I cringed at the sight of his thin wrist peeking from his too small, frayed pajama sleeves. They all needed new clothes, the oldest needing them most. They needed new bedding, too, but no one outside the house would see their torn, stained sheets and blankets, so those could wait. I didn't know where the money would come from to take care of those things. My babies never asked for anything—but the teachers at their school wouldn't extend me that same grace if I kept sending them with ripped clothes two sizes too small. Jamarcus would have told me they didn't need anything new right then. He had the privilege of not being the one Children's Protective Service would grill with an investigation, nor would he be especially upset if the boys were taken from us. I would die without my sons.

I kissed the three of them and replaced kicked off covers on the other two. Jamarcus would be done wolfing down his food soon, so I hurried into our bedroom. The door to the nightstand stood open and I kicked it shut, not wanting him to even glimpse the old massage paraphernalia visible inside. There would be no romantic massage that evening, or any evening. I should have thrown all that useless stuff in the trash long ago. I felt stupid for having thought I could salvage anything in the marriage by keeping it to use one day. That day was never coming.

There hadn't been a romantic moment between us for a very long time. I pulled off my clothes and put on the homeliest pajamas I owned, hoping to fend him off that night. He was most in the mood for the rough, quick sex that had become our staple coupling whenever he was in a foul mood like he was that night. I wasn't feeling it, and I didn't want to have to fight. I made my retreat to the hall bathroom, to wait him out.

I heard him banging around in the kitchen, throwing the chair against the table. Then, I was immersed in darkness. I'd hoped the light company would give us a reprieve.

"Dammit! You didn't pay the bill, Sasha?" I could hear more banging around. The boys slept with small battery-operated fans in their room, so I didn't worry about them waking up in the heat and noise.

Even in the dark, Jamarcus found his vodka. I could almost hear him taking long swallows straight from the bottle. I leaned against the tank of the toilet and hoped the roaches wouldn't rush out into the darkness until I'd already made it into bed. I pulled a candle out of the space saver above me and waited to light it.

After about twenty minutes, Jamarcus bustled his way to our room and threw himself down onto our bed. Nightly showering had also left his routine. I was glad I hadn't changed the sheets. He could sleep in his own funk.

Once I was sure he'd fallen asleep, I lit the candle and placed it on top of the shelf, so my babies could find their way to the bathroom during the night if they needed to.

I checked on the boys one last time and went to the hall closet and pulled down a blanket. I made sure it was one big enough to wrap my body in completely. Despite the heat, I'd be fine as long as Jamarcus couldn't touch me. Fighting his way through the blanket would be too much work for him, so I was pretty sure I'd be safe from his stick and jab that night.

I needed a good night sleep: I had to go see Shorty the next day.

"Hey, Sexy. It's about time you hollered at your boy." Shorty unfolded his six feet, seven inches of caramel from behind his desk and met me halfway across the room. He nodded at the dude who'd ushered me in, and the door was closed behind him.

He pressed full lips to my cheek, and then to my lips. I allowed him to hold onto my waist for a few moments longer than I probably should have, and then pulled away.

"Hey, Shorty." I'd planned exactly what I would say to my ex-lover, but the words escaped me.

"That fool acting up again?" He knew me well. The long lashes framing his eyes made them softer than I knew they were. I was the only person alive who knew what the gleam underneath those curtains meant. Anyone else who'd figured it out had done so too late.

I turned away from Shorty. "That's my husband. And my babies' daddy."

"Yeah, yeah. You all in love and shit." He pulled my chin back towards him with his finger. "But you're sad. Just say the word. I'll do his punk ass myself."

"It ain't like that, Shorty. Really." I still couldn't look him in the eyes. Jamarcus had lost his damned mind in the past couple of years, but I didn't want him iced. "I need some paper. Kinda short nowadays."

Shorty took one more squeeze of my waist and headed back to his desk. "I knew that poser wasn't handling his business." He slid out a drawer and pulled out stacks of cash. "How much you need, Sexy?"

I shifted my weight to the other side. "You know I'm not gonna just take money from you like that. I want to work for it. You got something or somebody for me to do?"

A different gleam shone from Shorty's eyes. "You mean like in the old days when we was partners in the streets?" He shook his head. "Um, um, um. You always were the best thing we had going for us." He dropped the money and leaned on the desk.

"We were always so good together, Baby. Why won't you just come on back to Daddy?"

I sighed. "We were good. But we were also dangerous." I remembered my time with Shorty. So did my body. Heat rose from between my thighs and I could smell my arousal. Shorty could too.

He closed his eyes and inhaled deeply. He stood as if to come back to where I was and I willed him to stop. I wasn't strong enough to resist him for long.

Finally, he sighed and sat down. "Go see this dude, Hakeem. He wants in and does pretty well, but I don't know yet if I can trust him. Break him down and give him a taste." He smiled. "Just let me know where his head is at. You wearing the sexy leather outfit?"

"You know it. Can't tell no lies when the garters are sliding across both sides of their heads."

Shorty scribbled an address on a slip of paper and brought it to me, sliding it down between my breasts. "I'll pay you four g's when you get back." He pressed a kiss to my right breast. "And if you come back early, I'll give you a bonus."

I backed away from him towards the door. My heart pounded, not just from his kiss, but from the excitement of finally being back in the game. I knew Shorty would come through for me and I wanted to get him what he asked for. I was so glad I had avoided Jamarcus's sex the night before. I couldn't be distracted from this job with him on my skin. My babies needed new clothes. Damn, I needed my lights turned back on, too.

"Shorty sent me to you, like a present, you know?" I pressed myself against the bulge in Hakeem's jeans.

He waved his boys away from the room. I straddled him on the table he leaned against and eased him down onto it.

"No shit? That mean I'm in?"

I swirled my tongue in his mouth before answering. "That depends on how you perform for me." I slid my skirt up above my hips and placed my thighs on each side of his head.

His cell phone rang, and he reached for it from his pocket, never taking his eyes off my thong clad mound.

"Yo, D, let me hit you back, man." He didn't wait for the caller to agree. The two seconds were all I'd needed to know who was on the phone. D was Shorty's biggest rival in those streets and the only reason Hakeem would be talking to him was if he was getting friendly with him—possibly working with him or sharing trade secrets—against Shorty.

"How you gonna answer your phone when you got all this booty in your face?" I slid my body down and dragged his arms up above his head and pinned him to the table. "That's rude."

He opened his mouth to protest, half smiling. I thrust my tongue into his mouth and coaxed his out to play. My fingernails lengthened into claws, and when his eyes shot open, I bit off his tongue.

My longer tongue slid from my nether lips and tore through the filmy leather of my panties. It wove its way through his jeans and entered his body. I lapped up his pain from his mouth, and held his legs in place with my extended, scaled toes. In my exuberance to be working again after so many years, I drank more than I should have, and I couldn't resist a few more bites than were necessary to finish him off.

Instead of taking the front door back out, I slid out the window that faced the back alley, affording myself a few more moments to savor my meal and pull myself back together.

Shorty had left by the time I returned to his office, but his boy handed me a fat envelope. I read the note. "I knew he was fucking off my money and trying to play me. Your bonus is inside, too."

I was happy to verify Shorty's feelings. And I'd been wanting that snack for ages. I rubbed my hands across the stack and headed to the electric company offices.

"The fuck you been, dressed like that?" I hadn't known Jamarcus would be home early. He'd beat the kids home from school.

"I had to go pay the light bill." I moved to get past him to go change clothes, but he blocked my way.

"Where'd you get the money?"

"I borrowed it." I tried again to move around him.

"Like hell you did. You been tricking all this time, while I've been working my ass off for you?"

I felt the familiar anger bubbling again. "You don't work for me; you work for you."

He grabbed my arm and threw me against the wall. He punched me in the stomach. Recent years had escalated the violence, but he'd never outright punched me like that before. He fumbled with his belt and the realization that he was aroused tore through me.

Pain clouded my vision and I could no longer remember that I loved him or that he was the father of my children. He hiked my skirt up and entered my body.

Instead of an opening, he was met with my own appendage. It swirled around him and slid into his penis. I jerked away from him and stabbed at him with the claws I hadn't felt slide out. My sharpened teeth slurred my words.

"I'm sick of your shit." I raked down his torso in one slash and pulled my tongue from his body and tightened it around his neck.

"I fix your fuck ups and I do without because of your selfishness. My babies don't have because you're such a dick." His face ballooned with pressure.

I wanted to feed on him, but his blood was sour, his flesh rancid. I left him with his blackness.

I called Shorty and he came to the house for me. He held me while I cried and his boys took care of what was left of Jamarcus.

"I lost control, Shorty. I've always been able to contain myself," I sobbed.

He caressed the scales on my back and brought my head up for a kiss. "It's okay, Baby. His days were numbered. Don't know how you kept from icing his punk ass this long."

"What do I tell the boys?"

"You tell them they got a new daddy who's gonna take care of them and raise them to be the special men they'll become when they grow into their powers. Y'all are coming home with me." He stroked my tongue and kissed it, too.

"He wasn't even worth eating." He spat out the residue of my ex-husband, and I felt my claws begin to retract.

"No rush, Baby," he said. "I got another job for you. We go in the back door on this one, so we can go just like this."

A Monster By Any Other Name

S he didn't have to die. When I told her we could live forever, she thought it was nineteen-year-old false bravado. She wasn't ready. Even in my ageless wisdom, I was drunk with weakness. The teenaged body I inhabited said it wanted her. We were to become parents.

The baby would be a boy. He talked to me as she carried him.

Will we all be together forever? He punctuated with a kick.

"I don't know." I tried to reassure him through a caress of her belly. I knew better and wanted to change the way things would play out. There was one chance.

Our son's naming ritual would seal his immortality. I had already given him my blood, and it would protect him as it had protected me. If we had completed the ritual, he would have been able to save his mother. I don't know that she was worth saving.

I'd hoped she would let us try. If the circle closed through his marking, he would come into his power immediately. He could heal her with a nip of his gums as he suckled at her breast, giving her what she would need to cheat death.

"We talked about his name while you carried him. Now that he's been here, I want him to carry this name. My name." This was necessary. For all of us.

"It's not fair. He should carry my name, too. I'm the one who did all the work to get him here."

I took my last look at her through a screen of tears. She would not survive until my return.

The cinema of her death assaulted me as I left the hospital.

She smirked, waited until I left the hospital room, and called the vital statistics clerk back for a change. A change we hadn't agreed on before I left. A change that would seal her death.

Her refusal to give our son my last name—as is tradition in this country, and as we'd agreed—meant he wouldn't come into his full existence yet. The legacy I had given him went beyond what she called toxic masculinity and the patriarchy.

She'd just learned those words from her mother, the older woman heatedly insisting the baby should be named for their family since we weren't married. They thought they knew everything, from their books. They already thought themselves much smarter than I.

What is in a name? A monster by any other name than the one my family chose eons ago and one his mother and I had not agreed on would not seal my son's identity. Our family name had to be willingly bestowed, formally recorded for validity by an outside authority. This was the modern equivalent to our ancient ceremonies, the ones that would unleash the full extent of his power, granted through our bloodline. He would only then, even in his infancy, inherit the gifts the power granted.

I was glad I wasn't there when she began to hemorrhage. They couldn't blame it on me. I watched her soul cry out, not knowing mine was there with her. It was only upon her last breath that she saw me and understood. Her shame was too late.

I returned to the hospital to retrieve my son. What's in a name? Identity. Eternity. Power. Salvation.

'Til Death Do Us Part

J immy Dean had loved me all his life. Least, that's what he told me when I was fourteen and he caught me behind Papa's barn and forced me to make love with him. He said he couldn't live without me and would love me until the day he died. Even after that. To marry him was the natural thing for me to do, even after he hit me in the jaw and broke a tooth when I wore a dress he didn't like to his parent's house for dinner. "I didn't mean to hurt you," he told me later. "I just love you so much. You know I don't like that ugly dress. You're supposed to do what I say. You belong to me. Always have and always will."

He used to like to re-tell the stories about the times I followed him through the wheat fields like a puppy, like he was a god. He never failed to mention how he was really good to let me follow him all those times, either. Paired with his declarations of undying love, I took these stories as a telling of my future and I married Jimmy.

Although my teachers always said I was bright and should attend the community college in the next town, I became a housewife instead. I was reasonably happy, too, just about as happy as the rest of the wives in our farm town. Jimmy always wanted his house clean, and he liked his breakfast, lunch, and dinner on the table, on time all the time. The big old rambling farmhouse his grandparents left us always made sure I had something to do between cooking and cleaning. But even with all the work I had to do every day, I still found some time to sneak into a corner of the kitchen and read my travel magazine.

I kept a fantasy of going to Los Angeles, California. The article in my magazine had the most wonderful pictures. The story was about taking a weekend getaway trip to the City of Angels, but I imagined that living there permanently must be heavenly, just the same. Australia would even be nice to visit, with all the water and smiling, friendly people and kangaroos.

I'd gotten really good at keeping this magazine hidden from Jimmy. He burned the last one I had after he caught me reading it in bed one afternoon. I was recovering from a miscarriage brought on by one of his rages at my refusing to have sex with him. "Jimmy," I'd said, "you know Doc said he was a little worried about me and the baby, and that I should take it kinda easy so we both do okay."

Jimmy pretended not to hear me and continued coming closer to me with that lustful look on his face. "Jimmy...no!"

He grabbed me and threw me backwards against the stove and tried to undo his belt buckle. I felt the searing pain in my lower back right before something ran from up inside me and down between my legs. The last thing I remembered was Jimmy pouring his own stickiness into me and then slapping me and telling me to get up and clean myself up.

Then I was in the hospital listening to some young doctor tell me that I could have some other kids some other time and not to do any heavy housework or have sex for four weeks. Doc, our elderly, regular doctor from town, came down to the house to see after me when Jimmy got me back home. He glared at Jimmy and looked like he could see through my head back to the night I lost the baby.

"Now Sarah, don't you do anything at all these next few weeks. Not anything at all." He stared pointedly at Jimmy over the rim of his glasses. "This includes that slave work you do as well as having sexual relations. Got that?"

I looked down at the cover as Jimmy's dark brown skin turned three different shades of red and he mumbled an answer, although Doc was supposedly addressing me. Then the old man turned to me.

"It is very important that your body recover from this strain. If you don't think you can get the rest you need here at home then I can take you back to town with me tonight." Now it was my turn to blush. Jimmy stared at me with those cold brown eyes and wordlessly dared me to go. I mumbled my own answer and watched the poor old doctor move toward the door, alone, shaking his head piteously.

All night that night and the next morning, Jimmy grumbled about having to make his own food. But he went out to the field at six that morning, just like every other morning, to do his work. I was relieved when he left and looked forward to the stillness of the house. I missed the baby already, although I had barely begun to feel it move. My grief lasted only the first day, until I realized that the baby and I were both better off that it hadn't been born to a father like Jimmy. I fearfully raised my eyes to the doorway of the bedroom, half expecting him to have heard my silent thanks. But of course, he didn't.

I was all alone with only a small black and white television for entertainment, but I didn't care. I would rather spend the day looking at my travel magazine anyway. I was so into the book that I failed to hear Jimmy's heavy footsteps come up the porch and into the room until he was standing right over me.

"You sorry bitch!" he roared as he snatched my magazine from my hands. He went to the stove and set the book on fire. Then he threw the flaming book onto my nightgown, and I frantically put out the fire. "I'm out there slaving in the heat after starving to death for the past few days and your lazy ass is laying in the bed like a damned queen reading some magazine."

He began to pick up the smoldering pages of the magazine and throw them at me once again. "When you ever think you're going anywhere? California is for people who have lives. Ain't but one place for sorry whores like you, and you're already there." Too late, I'd seen the look in his eyes and had no defense. Jimmy Jr. was born eight months later.

I loved my son. Jimmy couldn't seem to stop raving over how smart he was and how like him he was. I prayed that he wasn't and continued my daily chores. Jimmy Jr. was crazy about his daddy. Whenever Jimmy went out to the field in the mornings, Jimmy Jr. raised his chubby little arms and cooed to go along. After Jimmy explained that he couldn't and that he would return in the afternoon for lunch, the baby seemed to understand him and waited patiently for his daddy to return.

The last afternoon we spent at the farmhouse, Jimmy didn't come in from the fields for lunch. I found it rather strange, but I was relieved that I wouldn't have to scurry and jump about trying to do all the things he wanted me to do before he said them and swatted me.

Well past five o'clock, his usual dinner time, Jimmy came into the house. I immediately knew there was something wrong when all he said was, "Sarah, take me to bed."

I whirled around from the sink to face him and was startled to find that his face was completely colorless. He moved a little slower than usual, and he didn't have anything ugly to say to me. I helped him to make it to our bed and laid him down.

"Are you having dinner?" I asked, hesitantly.

"No. I'm not hungry." He seemed to have great difficulty moving his mouth. I didn't ask any more questions. I simply removed his clothes before he could decide that that was what I needed to do next. The large purplish bruises startled me. I met his eyes. They seemed to have grown even colder, as translucent brown as that tiger eye jewelry some of the women in my magazine wore. I didn't ask any more questions. I returned to the kitchen to play quietly with Jimmy Jr. An hour or so later, Jimmy called to me.

"Sarah. Bring Jr. for me to play with him." The words came slowly. I obediently picked our son up and took him to the bedroom. Jimmy could not move quickly enough to take the baby from my arms. I gently laid the baby in the crook of his daddy's arm. Jimmy Jr. began to scream at the top of his lungs. I snatched him back up, to examine him for diaper pins or straggling ants in his diaper but found nothing. The baby continued to scream in terror.

Jimmy looked up at us, as if he wanted to reach out to the baby, but he couldn't raise his arm. It was obvious that Jimmy Jr. didn't want anything to do with Jimmy. Finally, I told him that Jimmy Jr. was probably just tired and I'd put him to bed early.

After setting the baby down for bed, I changed into my nightgown. Jimmy's position on the bed hadn't changed, but his eyes stared out coldly from his face. The large bruises I found on his back had spread to his side. I climbed into bed. During the night I was awakened by a tight feeling around my chest. I felt Jimmy prodding me from the back with his penis. "I want you to do all the work this time. I don't feel so good."

I moved the way I knew he liked me to, hoping that he would climax quickly and take his arms from around me. After thirty minutes of moving and wiggling, I was sore. And I felt like I couldn't breathe. His erection would not go down.

"Jimmy, please let me go." The only answer I got was a gurgling sound. Frantically, I struggled to free myself, finally managing to squeeze out from between his arms and onto the floor. I turned on the light. Jimmy had grown paler, more ashen. His body remained rigidly still in the bed, but his eyes flashed wintry threats at me.

His voice, just as cold, came out as a harsh whisper. "You belong to me."

Suddenly, I knew that something was terribly wrong with Jimmy. I hurriedly ran to the top of the closet and took the money out that Jimmy stashed away for lean times. I was shocked to find there were a few thousand dollars in the can. I only had moments to give free rein to the anger charging through me at how much I'd gone without, how much

Jimmy had made sure the baby and I didn't have, while he stashed money away like that. Knowing him like I did, Jimmy probably didn't even have any plan for the money—except to keep it away from me.

Unless it had been him planning for a life that didn't include me.

I shivered and then dressed and packed the few decent items of clothing I had. The entire time, I felt chills down my spine as the frosty daggers were being shot at me. I whirled around to make sure that Jimmy wasn't coming after me.

He wasn't. His icy gaze was focused on my treasured travel magazine sticking out from between the seat of the chair in the room. I knew he wanted to say or do something but couldn't. I rushed into the baby's room and got him ready to go. The last thing I did was write a note for Doc, asking him to look in on Jimmy and make any arrangements that needed to be made for him, which I took into town on my way down the road.

I remember being grateful that Jimmy had insisted on teaching me to drive the old pickup a few years ago so that I could help him out with his chores sometimes. I knew exactly where I was headed.

A year later, my son and I were doing just fine in the sunny California. I'd found a nice old lady to keep Jimmy Jr. and I had a job as a typist in a rather large insurance company. The pay wasn't much, but with the money I'd brought, Jimmy Jr. and I were comfortable and had a little money saved. More than a thousand miles from home and I was finally free in my City of Angels.

Until the day I saw the man standing outside the building where I worked. I ran past him as I made my way into the building and raced to my desk. Icy prickles began to tiptoe up my back as I pulled open the blinds to my cubicle. "That man couldn't possibly be looking at me. I don't know anybody here and I'm way up on the fifteenth floor."

But the chills proved me wrong. I felt more than saw icy eyes that were once brown, staring directly at me, burning so brightly that the fifteen floors felt less than fifteen inches. I told my boss that I was feeling ill and needed to go home. As I raced past the man on the street, he turned ever so slowly to face me.

He moved with a wobbling gate, as if he didn't have any control over his body and could only move in slow jerky movements. The dark suit that hadn't needed washing very often because it was the church suit was out of season in the modern sunny city. His stench turned the noses of even the most seasoned city dwellers, used to the rancid odor of pollution and whatnot.

I ran the entire three blocks to the bus stop. By the time the bus came, he'd managed to turn completely around in the spot where he stood and his white brown gaze burned my soul and followed me onto the bus.

I didn't have to hear the words to understand what he slowly mouthed. "You belong to me."

I rushed up the stairs to relieve the babysitter. I only lived about three miles from my job. How did he find us? Covering twelve hundred miles in a year meant that in about another day or so he would be here at the house. I started throwing our meager belongings into our luggage.

Australia was usually nice this time of year.

Soulmates

S he wasn't sure who had chosen that suit for him for burial but whether it was his side chick or his nosy mother, the bitch had done a perfect job.

Leticia ran her hands lovingly down Damien's chest, remembering how well the burgundy suit had fit him when he was alive. Even in death, he cut a fine figure in his casket, sharp suit and burgundy pimp hat with the black feather band, pulled down to the left side, just like he liked it. He had known it made him look like a real live pimp and she guessed that was a more honest description of him than she would have ever admitted out loud.

Whoever the mortuary had doing hair and make-up must have been used to doing Black folks' hair and faces because her beloved looked like he was about to open his eyes and step out of the casket. His dark brown skin looked life like, painted a color closer to living flesh than his three weeks dead body could have displayed without the artist's artistic experience. His locs flowed perfectly down his shoulders, moisturized just right to where the scent of coconut oil still lingered above his casket. They done good.

He didn't look like a dead guy who had been killed by his dead girlfriend.

Not wanting to wear out her welcome in those wee hours of the morning and be discovered by staff opening up for the day's business, or overeager mourners arriving early to get visitations and services out of the way as soon as possible, Leticia patted Damien's hard, cold cheek and whispered her promise into the quiet of the chapel.

"I'll be waiting for you at home."

She moved swiftly, unencumbered by the embalming fluid and autopsy that would probably slow Damien down when he first came back to her. They'd have to figure out how to help him work around those issues. They had plenty of time. Like she'd told him the last time they saw each other, they were bonded and neither of them was going anywhere without the other.

Leticia chose her favorite chair in front of the television at their house, where she could see the door clearly. She didn't need to sleep. She hoped Damien would arrive shortly after his burial but she knew it could take him a bit of time to get oriented enough to come on back to the house. She didn't need to eat, either, so she could wait for as long as she needed for their reunion.

She propped her legs up on the coffee table, examining the bruises on her pale legs, settled into pooled spots on her shins from when Damien had lain her, face down, in a shallow grave out in the dump yard behind the projects they lived in. Those marks were easy enough to cover. The ones on her throat where he'd choked her out until she breathed her last breath, not so much. Leticia was just glad decay hadn't set in as fully as it could have before she had clawed her way up through the broken glass and discarded bicycle tires to trample through the garbage and get back to her beloved.

"He never listened to me when I told him I wasn't like other women." She shook her head and sucked her teeth. Damien had thought she was just flexing, trying to cement her positioning as wifey and pin him down. She'd told him some variation of the same throughout their eight-year, tumultuous relationship, throughout which he evaded committing fully to her and marrying her.

There were other ways to bond yourself to someone. He couldn't get away from her if he tried.

They might have fought violently every other month and cheated on each other even more frequently than that. He may have been unwilling to turn in his player card and quit the game. Women of varying ages, ethnicities, and classes may have thrown themselves on him at every turn, with him taking full advantage of the ample selection. None of that mattered because Leticia loved him. He was hers. And she wasn't some common chick, living a common life, doing common shit.

No flex. Real talk.

In her heart of hearts, she knew he was unconvinced she was the best thing to ever happen to him. Why else would he leave her hanging on a string, even after she had contrived a financial problem that required that they live together so she could show him, first hand, her domestic skills? Why hadn't he felt the need to at least propose to her after any one of her numerous "miscarriages"?

He had just needed a little help. Leticia went to find the practitioner on the outskirts of the 'hood to provide the kind of assistance he wouldn't be able to figure out or resist.

"Do you understand what you asking me to do, child?" The old woman had peered at her over the top of her thin, wire framed glasses. I done heard about you and your Damien. Ain't no commitment there because ain't no real love there." She sucked her teeth and turned back to face the work-table at her side.

"We do love each other. We just lose sight of that sometimes." Leticia was annoyed at the woman. But she needed her help so she held her tongue.

At that, the woman threw her head back and belly laughed. "Ya lose sight of it because you like being blind. You can't magic somebody into loving you without at least a foundation of that love in the first place. You asking me to do something that will come at a much higher cost than the regular love spells."

"I don't care about the cost. I'll pay anything." Leticia reached for her wallet inside her purse as the old lady guffawed again.

"I know you got money from some other man to pay for this. Imma take your dirty money. Understand this, though, girl: you may not get what you think you want, in the way you want to have it."

Leticia had reached the end of her patience. "Whatever. Just tell me what to do."

She repeated the words, took the powder, left her offerings, and went home to fix dinner.

Damien hadn't even come home in time for dinner that night. Although he had gone straight to the shower and stayed for a long time, she still smelled another woman's essence on his skin. Panicked, she rubbed the powder into the juncture of her thighs. No matter how much sex they had with other people, Leticia and Damien couldn't stay away from each other. She made sure he took in all the powder she offered from her body. When he lay next to her, exhausted from the physical exertion he had participated in that day, she whispered the last words to put her love spell into effect. She loved him and he loved her. Nothing would change that.

Even after he had killed her during their penultimate argument when he'd found out her latest conquest had been his closest homeboy, she had still loved him. Her affairs to that point had been quiet, with Leticia smiling to herself when she watched Damien crawl into their bed at night, thinking he was getting away with something with his serial cheating.

That entanglement with Toad had caught him wrong, though. Enraged that she dared do the exact same things he was doing, and with his homeboy, at that, he had wrapped his large hands around her throat and choked her out.

At least he'd cried as he carried her body out of their house and took her to the dump to bury her. She heard his gut wrenching sobs as he worked. He had loved her. He just hadn't known how to do it in a healthy way. Neither of them had understood how to maintain a healthy relationship with each other. They'd have to work towards that when they got back together.

She had caught him by surprise when she came back in through their back door a few days later, all the color draining from his face as he took in her disheveled appearance and apparent return from death. Leticia had tried to explain to him then that they could never be separated and that she forgave him for killing her. She hadn't had the chance to say all that when she saw he had been preparing their home for another woman to come into for the night.

She went into the kitchen and grabbed the biggest knife they had and commenced to stabbing him to death. Her motions quickly morphed into the same rhythm and direction of the words and melody of the booty song he had playing through the speakers. She stabbed him up and down and round and round until he was a bloody mess. Then, before she left his body there to be found by the other woman, Leticia whispered into his ear with a rush of a dead breath she no longer needed to take.

"I'll see you again, soon, Beloved."

That was all it had taken for his journey back to her to begin. Her breath would take him through his burial, his re-awakening, and his return home. To her. Their bond would never end, no matter how many lives they had to live. Their dead bodies could always be buried but their love could never die. It would resurrect every time. Both Leticia and Damien would always return to the land of the living to be with one another, eternally bonded to their beloved.

Leticia waited days for Damien to return, then a couple of weeks. Just when she thought she would have to go search his gravesite, the front door creaked as someone jiggled a key in the lock. Damien wouldn't have used a key. Leticia hid in the hallway closet, peering through the small crack she left in the door. She watched as a woman came inside the house and shut the door behind her, with silent tears becoming harsh sobs as soon as the door was closed.

"I still feel you everywhere. I think I see you every time I turn around. And I miss you so much. Why did you leave me?" She collapsed onto the floor of the foyer and continued to cry until her body shook from the force of her grief.

"The nerve of this bitch, coming into my damned house like she's supposed to be here!" Leticia was hotter than fish grease at the invasion. The woman was apparently heartbroken but rather than elicit sympathy from Leticia for them having loved the same man, Leticia just wanted to get rid of the other woman. Permanently.

She threw the closet door open and approached the woman on the floor, who did not notice her until she stood directly above her.

"You really taking your job as homewrecker to the extreme, ain't you?" Leticia kicked the woman in the side of her face and knocked her into a prone position on the floor. "Why are you here? Why were you ever here? He's mine. Forever."

She wrapped her hands around the woman's neck and banged her head repeatedly into the hardwood floor while she choked her. A large pool of blood formed underneath them and still, Leticia pressed down hard on her neck. She did not stop until a gravelly gasp emerged from the direction of the kitchen.

"No!" Damien whispered the word across decaying vocal cords and ambled towards the two women.

Leticia rose to greet Damien. "Baby, I'm so glad to see you." She opened her arms for an embrace and Damien pushed her to the side and knelt beside the woman she had killed.

"No! I love you. I have always loved you. I've been following you around and standing outside your house, trying to figure out how to tell you I came back. Don't leave me."

Leticia's dead heart broke at hearing the words Damien was saying to the other woman's corpse.

"Damien, she's not important. I'm your soul mate. Let's go and start our next life together." She took a step towards him and stopped with his next words, spoken into the dead woman's ear.

"I'll see you again soon, Beloved. Return to me."

Shock coursed through Leticia as the woman slowly began to move again. Damien smiled, torn lips highlighting his grotesque joy.

"What happened, Damien?"

"I couldn't live without you and now we can live together forever."

Unable to witness their love any longer, Leticia ran out the kitchen door Damien had recently come into. She wanted to cry but her tear ducts no longer worked like that. She replayed everything in her mind trying to figure out where she had gone wrong. She had done everything the old woman told her to do. Said everything she was supposed to say. Then she understood. It had been the powder.

Oh, she was so smart, being creative with the powder. That dirty mother fucker must have run straight to that bitch with the powder still on his lips and his body. And he loved his side chick. She loved him. That shit bonded them together. Forever. She couldn't kill them again because they'd just get back up and love each other some more. She had fucked up and got a raw deal with that magic shit.

What the hell was she gonna do for an eternity of immortality, dead and all alone?

An Old-Fashioned Type of Girl

Mama always told her to get to a man's heart through his stomach, but it was Granny who taught her how to put in that little something extra to make sure they stuck around.

Charla stirred the batter carefully, mimicking the slow roll of a stand mixer. She had one of those fancy things, but she only used it on certain holidays or when she was pressed for time—never when she was baking her signature Forever Cake. She sighed. She'd made this same cake six different times in the past year and a half. She wanted this to be the last time she made it as an unmarried woman.

Charla was born to be a wife. Mama and Granny had carefully trained her in all wifely duties, especially cooking, housekeeping, and carrying herself as a respectful lady at all times. Granny left most of the lady lessons to Mama because Granny was no lady and didn't think a woman had to do that "silly play-acting" to get herself hitched. So Mama taught her how to apply make-up so artfully it didn't look like you had any on and how to speak and laugh demurely. She also taught Charla to have a general interest in most things but never too much knowledge about one thing, except making men happy.

Men loved that she took an interest in the things they liked but that she wasn't smarter than they were. Charla learned at a young age that she actually was smarter than most of the men she met. She just never let them know. They also loved her 1960s aesthetic. She always wore her hair in a simple and sleek style, reminiscent of Diana Ross' flipped bob from when she sang with The Supremes. Mama always said, "Fads are trite and they change so you need to be timeless." Her beautician was in the old neighborhood, an elderly lady who declared she'd keel over and die in her shop before she'd quit. Ms. Bessie understood that Charla was special and kept her fittingly coiffed.

Charla never wore pants, only dresses. And always with pumps. Not the six-inch styles that were in fashion, but the four-inch ones that always made a soft and graceful line of her calves. She might have considered pants for when she had to do dirty, outside work, but men loved doing things for Charla. She had a lawn man who kept her yard beautiful, a mechanic who made sure she never had to even put air in her own tires, and a handyman that fixed everything he thought might break down before the next time he came over. But none of those men could marry her and Charla needed a husband.

So she dated. Not from online like other people. She only dated men she met at the supermarket or the bookstore. They got bonus points if they told her she was pretty, even if they compared her to Jackie O. She was more like Ann Lowe, thank you very much, whose selectivity helped her become the first highly sought Black fashion designer. Charla had farsighted, genius vision like Ms. Lowe and she used it all the time. The fast talkers who admired her small waist, big hips, and smooth, dark skin were usually after only one thing. And the one who married her could have that one thing. All the temporary fly-by-nights couldn't even consider sniffing it.

That's the most important part of what Granny taught her about cooking and courting: give them a food test before you tried to commit. She taught Charla how to put a little of herself into one specialty dish to present to a man she thought she might want to marry. How he reacted to that dish would tell the tale. All men wanted you to cook for them and pamper them but only the man made for you would get a particular twinkle in his eye as he ate what you prepared. He'd let you know he tasted the effort you put into the dish. Only then should Charla plan to be with her forever husband.

Most men failed the test. If a man stuck around long enough for the two-month mark, Charla would invite him to her home for a meal. If he progressed past that, she invited him again the next week. Some of the men never made it past the first meal. They'd gobble her food down with poor manners and not offer any compliments beyond unbuckling their belts because they'd gorged themselves. They farted and belched. They tried to take off their clothes because they thought being inside her home meant she wanted to have sex with them. Charla had to give those men the quick exit, without any more of her exquisite cooking. Others made it to the second week only to do something rude like, announce, "You'll make some lucky man a good wife." That meant he'd take all the benefits but never wife her. Or they simply collapsed at the table, their transformation beginning with crackling joints and grunted rebukes before their ability to speak was taken away. They weren't strong enough.

Charla really hoped the man she was making the cake for was as special as she felt he was. She was an old-fashioned type of girl but he made her feel supremely unladylike, in the most delicious and decadent ways. She rubbed her hand across her belly, gasping as her core contracted at her thoughts and touch. She slowly untucked her blouse from her skirt and pinched a generous amount of her waist flesh. The tissue came loose in her fingers. She winced. That part hurt but it was worth it. She put it in the clay mortar Granny had gifted her and ground the quickly drying flesh with the pestle. The colors and faintly metallic odor never grew any less fascinating to her.

Granny made sure she understood how extraordinary the two of them were. Their bloodline provided them benefits that could come in handy. For Granny, the gift was that of sight. Granny always knew when things would happen. She even foretold her own death—that's why she started her lessons with Charla so early. Mama hadn't gotten any gift, so Granny had never told her about theirs. Charla's gift was the little something she always put into her Forever Cake. It hadn't steered her wrong yet.

A piercing mewl carried up from the basement and Charla furrowed her brow. She needed to feed the babies before her date arrived so they'd stay calm and quiet. She never introduced them to her dates. There was no point in that if the men wouldn't be sticking around to play Daddy. She took the mortar with her to the basement stairs. Charla heard halted thudding on the stairs as the little ones bumbled upwards.

"Mommy's here, sweetlings," she cooed as she opened the door. She stirred her now powered flesh in the bowl with her finger and then poured it into her palm. Soft tongues dipped into her hand. She didn't make a habit of feeding them her flesh on a regular basis. She didn't want them to grow spoiled. The flesh of others kept them sustained. Sometimes, animals would do. Other times, they needed more, and she gave it to them.

The one called Patrick slithered up closest to her and she stroked his knotted head. She'd really liked Patrick and she just knew two months ago that he was the one. He wasn't. One bite of her Forever Cake and his transformation was instantaneous. She'd cried over that one as she carried him down to the basement to place him with her other failed dates. Fred growled in the corner furthest away from her. He'd been there the longest, the meanest and the most unfit to be her husband. His transformation had been slow and torturous. Even now, months later, he was still changing, his flesh bulging and oozing as it shifted. No wonder he had such a bad attitude.

He needed her to take care of him now. All of them did. Her babies. They were her creations, of her flesh. Of her gift. She had to take care of them until they expired. When her husband came along, he wouldn't change like the others. He would be fortified by her Forever Cake, stronger and invincible. The joining of her ancient flesh and his would be exquisite, even before they commenced on their physical relationship. Then they'd be married so she could have help taking care of her progeny.

"Mommy has to get us a Daddy. Be sweet now, and hush up so we can talk." The mewling stopped and slow thumping indicated her babies were going back down the stairs to do her bidding. Too bad they hadn't all been that sweet or obedient before they'd changed over.

When she arrived back in the kitchen, she pinched another section of dark brown flesh from her waist and began the work of grinding it into powder again. She poured it into the main mixing bowl and began the slow rolling mixing motions again. Charla carefully scraped the mix into the prepared pans. She placed the cake in the oven. It looked perfect. This man had to be the one. She didn't need any more babies.

Besides, who knew how much tinier her waist could get without her starting to look unnatural? People might get suspicious and think she was some kind of monster or something.

Into the Nothingness

Ice covered the lake like white film on a corpse's eyes. I made out swirling patterns I wanted to pretend were the water, still alive beneath the nothingness. Nevertheless, I knew better. Nothing could survive the wrath of the snow, ice, and freezing temperatures. Nothing could survive the encompassing whiteness.

I had a friend who was a social worker who claimed to turn off her "diagnosing super powers" when dealing with her friends on a personal level but really didn't. She had told me directly, "It's just snow. It happens all the time in other parts of the country. You're simply afraid of new things, and going to graduate school is the unknown you're actually afraid of. And even though you ought to be used to it by now, you're a little afraid of being one of the few black bodies on that campus."

She was wrong. The snow was *wrong*.

Despite what my sister friend said, I wasn't afraid of being the only black person on campus. I didn't run into very many writers of color in the rest of my world so I figured that was part of the game in academia, too. I'd already learned how to deal with my double minority status in higher education.

What I wasn't prepared for was the boundless blanket of white covering everything miles below the aircraft. Even from our flying height, there were miles and miles of blank emptiness. The stark landscape was interrupted every so often by a gray, lifeless structure, or a dingy, barely visible plowed road through the ice. I was amazed at how much detail I could see from the window despite the snow disappearing everything.

I grabbed my cell when the plane slid into the gate at O'Hare to pick up more passengers. I turned it on and sent a quick text.

"The snow has taken the airport hostage. Looks like a beach of white." That was the only thing I could liken my alien view to, having at least seen what passes for a beach in Texas. The airport did have the infinity of the sand and sea, the white blanket of snow all that existed between the airplanes on the tarmac and beyond.

Making my final landing did nothing to improve my outlook. A slightly familiar but mostly foreign anxiety bubbled up inside my throat.

I walked outside to the shuttle bus and cold sank into my bones my bones. I welcomed the opposition to the humid seventy-degree weather Houston called winter. However, the frigid ache gripped my teeth, and sent my wide, welcoming Southern smile into hiding. I wanted to hide, too, but couldn't. My dark brown skin stood out against the backdrop of white snow, white people, and white white.

I holed up for the night in a stifling hot hotel room. Apparently, winter there meant that everyone between Pittsburgh and the college campus was freezing and needed to blast the heat. I turned on the air conditioning so I could breathe and stop my body from emulsifying. The artificial air wouldn't be much better, and I'd probably pay for it with some type of sinus upset. I could already feel my skin and hair dehydrating. Despite all the wet snow surrounding me, I could still dry up and blow away.

I flipped to the weather channel. *Didn't that beat all.* The area was expecting the most snowfall it had seen in several years. Obviously, because I had come to town. It seemed about right that Northern Mother Nature would decide to show out since I was visiting. I only wished I were really that important. But being a mere mortal, instead, I settled into bed, half under the covers and half out, falling asleep to the rhythm of snowflakes shadow dancing against the window.

The next morning found me staring out the same window, marveling at how the snow was still there. I could not have said where I'd expected it to go. It just seemed so...permanent. Elementary school science nipped at the back of my brain. As long as the temperature stayed below thirty-two degrees, the ice would not melt.

There was no way I would even attempt to drive in the alien terrain. I bummed a ride with another student headed to the campus and took in more of the dead world beneath the chilling blanket that extinguished everything else. The snow was falling again, and on the walk up the hill to the campus, the flakes skittered across my face and hands like tiny chilled feet. I laughed at the fluttery, tickly dance, and then the iciness slicing through my tooth fillings painfully reminded me I could not walk outside with my mouth open. I smiled with tight lips and bent to touch the fallen performers. They melted on contact and an unexpected sadness overcame me at having caused the demise of such cheerful creatures. A classmate suggested I get gloves to further my examination, and I was thankful for the advice.

The creatures lasted longer atop my gloved hands, and I squinted to identify the distinct crystals that made up each flake. All I saw were tiny clumps of ice. The clumps looked larger when pressed together, binding in a way that I found fascinating.

I brushed the remnants from my hands and tipped across the campus yard as quickly as I dared in my cowboy boots. I had been thinking warmth and comfort when I'd packed the Texan stereotypes, not traction. Falling was more than a mere possibility with all the ice and snow. I walked on the outside of an overturned bench. I wondered why the bench was flipped over but then decided the weight of the snow must have tipped it. The snow had piled up on both sides of the now vertical seat and covered the back where it lay on the ground. It was threatening to cover the entire bench. Small blue spheres lined the nearby sidewalk and the snow seemed to retreat from them. There were no blue circles around the bench.

I was running behind for class, but I had to know what the whole scenario with the bench was about. I waved to the first person I saw. "Hi. What's that blue stuff?"

His eyes crinkled up and his smile stayed just below an outright laugh. "The blue stuff on the ground?"

I nodded.

"That's salt."

"Salt?"

"Yep. It keeps the snow off the sidewalks and the roads."

"How does it do that? Is it a chemical reaction?"

This time he did laugh. "You're not from around here?"

I returned his smile. "No. I have never seen such a thing as all this white. And this blue."

"It's something like a chemical reaction that keeps the ice from building up on the places we need to get around town." He shrugged his shoulders. "Keeps roads and sidewalks clear of ice. Not magic, simple chemistry."

"Thanks. Now I know how this snow stuff works." I turned to leave and his laugh followed me into the building.

I took a seat next to the window in class and remained mesmerized by the weather. The snow fell non-stop for the couple of hours I was supposed to be learning the craft of storytelling. Apparently, I was also supposed to learn that describing a Black man's haircut as a fade was a no-no, because people unfamiliar with the Black experience wouldn't know what I meant. How was I supposed to tell my own stories, in my own voice, if they were to be void of my Black experiences? I felt the tug of erasure as the workshop droned on around me. I tuned everything out after the censure for writing about my authentic self.

I was already spinning another authentic story. The snow was a creature. It created and lived in a cold, bleak world, not allowing for any other existences than its own. And it took over everything in that world, eventually, because it was indestructible. It existed to erase all life beneath it: to obliterate anything outside of its whiteness.

The snow fell on the massive school building, covering the entire spired top and slanting down the slopes to the ground around the building. Within a couple of hours, the grounds were covered with several inches of snow. The view was pretty in its sparkly white, where the waning sun made glitter between the crystals. My mind went to wonderlands sang of in blissful songs. And to the murderous deadness of winter.

During our first break, someone suggested sledding down the big hill in front of the campus on lunch trays. My heart thudded at the thought of placing my body any more fully in the snow, and I was ecstatic when the idea was talked down. Nevertheless, curiosity drew me to the ice, where I could watch from a safe distance. It felt like it didn't want me there, but I resisted and existed, anyway. I walked outside, onto the patio. Further examination of the flakes found them to be light and airy, so the piles they made were higher than they would have been if the ice were compact.

I'd have thought I would feel better about the light snow, rather than a heavy onslaught, but the whole thing felt off in a way I could not explain. I leaned on the gate that surrounded the veranda and looked over into the back courtyard where I had come in. A larger white expanse covered the yard than there had been that morning. The snow crept to where we were in the main academic building, closer to the front doors. Where I had thought we were safe inside.

I returned to class and sat at the front so I could not be distracted by what was going on outside the school with the weather. I managed to concentrate during the last part of the day. The entire class time had not been wasted with me stinging from the earlier rebuke of my hairstyle terminology and daydreaming out the window.

We all packed up to go to dinner, but I stayed behind so I could have my mentor meeting. All I needed was a quick snack from the bookstore. Everybody jetted off quickly and the campus felt extra desolate in the cold, dark night. The moon already shone high in the clear sky and the air smelled of frost. No playful nipping of noses, only the sharp bite of icy teeth.

I took tentative steps onto the sidewalk heading towards the bookstore. Two other benches lay on their sides, already covered in snow. Three lumps of white stood where upright benches had been. I tipped slowly along the sidewalk. The blue lines had grown closer together and I felt like a model on a catwalk, trying to get my feet within the blue lines that made up less than half the sidewalk. Behind the new salt lines were new snow formations.

The bookstore was closed and I peered out at the sidewalk that would take me around the courtyard and to the library. I could get there much faster if I cut across the yard. I took a slow step onto the snow on the sides of the sidewalk. My foot sank as if inside a stale marshmallow, slightly crunchy and squeaky on the outside but squishy on the inside. The feeling was unsettling, but still I proceeded. My next step fell into a section of ice that was even softer. Steadily, I made my way to the middle of the yard, halfway to the library. I glanced at the landscaping alongside me and my next step took me sliding directly into it. For long moments, I could not catch my breath as I lay flat on my back. *I shouldn't have left the sidewalk.*

The snowflakes began their wild dance across my face and my uncovered neck. Fluttery before, the routine was harder this time, more purposeful. I felt each individual step they took onto my skin, harsh and pounding. I struggled to wipe the ice off my face, but more crystals covered the areas I wiped. They came down into my mouth and my eyes, until

I closed them both. The heat of my body did not melt the flakes. Instead, they expanded and covered my throat and marched down into my esophagus and through to my stomach.

I gagged, but I could not expel the ice. I willed my arms to move so I could turn myself over, but the appendages couldn't obey from underneath the flakes that covered them and pinned them down. As my stomach froze from the inside out, and my breath burst out of my nose in short, frosted spurts, I understood the mistake I had made.

I should have stayed on the sidewalk, inside my own lane. Although the snow was pushing its way through the markings, the salt *was* magical, having been used for millennia to defend against unearthly creatures and the obliteration of civilizations. Old magic. Yet, all it could do was buy us precious little time to escape to a place that would take longer to invade. Someone else may not have realized the snow was alive, but I had. I'd known it when I'd first seen the devouring blankness from the airplane. It's emulsification of the living had been the backdrop of my entire life.

How had I expected to live beside or within the void, when everything would eventually wind up beneath it? My thoughts grew hazy, fuzzy on the edges like the frost on the window of a warm room. There was no more warmth for me. Frozen and broken, I faded into the nothingness.

Acknowledgements

This collection wouldn't exist if not for the sheer will of my brother in writing, Gabino Iglesias. I uttered a non-commit, and you made sure I stuck to it. Thank you. And to Sarah and Rob at The Seventh Terrace, I couldn't have asked for a more positive and inspirational experience with my first collection. Thank you.

About the Author

Rhonda Jackson Garcia, AKA RJ Joseph, is a Stoker Award™ nominated, Texas based academic and creative writer/professor whose writing regularly focuses on the intersections of gender and race in the horror and romance genres and popular culture. She has had works published in various applauded venues, including the 2020 Halloween issue of *Southwest Review* and *The Streaming of Hill House: Essays on the Haunting Netflix Series*. Rhonda is also an instructor at the Speculative Fiction academy.

When she isn't writing, reading, or teaching, she can usually be found wrangling her huge blended family of one husband, four adult sprouts, seven teenaged sproutlings, four grandboo seedlings, and one furry hellbeast who sometimes pretends to be a dog.

She occasionally peeks out on Twitter @rjacksonjoseph or at www.rhondajacksonjoseph.com

Publication Credits

"Left Hand Torment", published February 14, 2018 by Mocha Memoirs Press, LLC in *Black Magic Women*

"Mamas Babies", published October 9, 2017 by Eakin Press in *Road Kill: Texas Horror by Texas Writers Volume 2*

"A Woman's Work", published May 15, 2017 by Sanguine Press in *Transitions and Awakenings: No Regrets*

"To Give Her Whatsoever She May Ask", Published March 10, 2017 by Cedar Grove Publishing in *Sycorax's Daughters*

"Bloodline", published March 2004 by Nocturnal Ooze Web Magazine

"Bloodline", published October 11, 2015 by Tea and a Tome Publishing in *Monstrous Domesticity*

"Bloodline", published July 2020 by Fright Girl Summer on www.frightgirlsummer.com

"Flesh of my Flesh", published October 11, 2015 by Tea and a Tome Publishing in *Monstrous Domesticity*

"Till Death Do Us Part", published October 11, 2015 by Tea and a Tome Publishing in *Monstrous Domesticity*

"Paid in Full", published August 5, 2012 by Hazard Yet Forward Project in cooperation with Evergreen Syndicate in *Hazard Yet Forward*

"Old-Fashioned Type of Girl", published November 30, 2020 by Sliced Up Press in *Slashertorte: An Anthology of Cake Horror*

"Conflict Resolution", published October 2020 in *Southwest Review*

"Conflict Resolution", performed February 2022, on *Nightlight Podcast*

"I Would Have Rescued Them All", published December 31, 2020 by Cemetery Gates Media in *Campfire Macabre*

"I Would Have Rescued Them All", performed February 2022 on *Something Scary*

"I Want to be Free", published March 16, 2021 by Cemetery Gates Media in *Paranormal Contact: A Quiet Horror Confessional*

"Soulmates", published September 2021 by Dark Dispatch in *Issue 2: Deadly Love*

The Seventh Terrace

Visit us online at
www.the-seventh-terrace.com

Additional Titles from The Seventh Terrace

CPSIA information can be obtained
at www.ICGtesting.com
Printed in the USA
LVHW040245260722
724372LV00004B/56